More praise for
The Dreams of Mairhe Mehan

◆"In this haunting, eloquent story, the barriers between inner and outer vision dissolve as a young immigrant loses the men she holds dear during the Civil War. Armstrong mixes vision and reality with breathtaking virtuosity, salting Mairhe's narrative with poetic turns of phrase, snatches of song, story, and history."

—*Kirkus Reviews*, Pointer

★"Artfully melding Mairhe's mundane and dream worlds, Armstrong offers the battle-weary genre of Civil War fiction a fresh and challenging new twist. The cast of fictional characters is vividly realized, and the stellar Walt Whitman shines."

—*The Bulletin*, Starred

★"Exploring an aspect of the immigrant experience, Armstrong's finely wrought historical novel also captures a powerful measure of the magnitude and depth of the pain caused by the Civil War. This novel is remarkable for its artistry and the lingering musicality of its language."

—*Publishers Weekly*, Starred

PRAISE FOR
Mary Mehan Awake

WINNER OF THE 1998 PATERSON PRIZE FOR BOOKS FOR YOUNG PEOPLE

Finalist for the Great Lakes Book Award

"Armstrong's prose is a marvel of economy and grace, with a lyrical quality that is unmatched."

—*The Buffalo News*

"Set in a time when America sought both healing and westward expansion, this story is about recovery and expanding horizons. A wonderful story about love, dreams, and renewal, written in beautiful prose."

—*School Library Journal*

"The story unfolds effortlessly and richly. It's *The Secret Garden* for an older audience, with friendship and nature gratifyingly providing healing and wholeness."

—*The Horn Book Magazine*

"The powerful use of imagery that distinguished Armstrong's previous novel is also much in evidence here."

—*The Bulletin*

To Mrs. Muller's Class

JENNIFER ARMSTRONG

Becoming Mary Mehan

TWO NOVELS

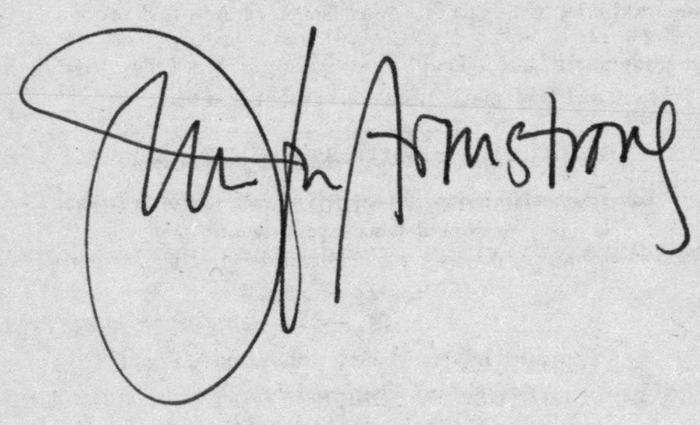

Published by Dell Laurel-Leaf, an imprint of Random House Children's Books, a division of Random House, Inc., 1540 Broadway, New York, New York 10036

The excerpt from Walt Whitman's poetry on page 131 is taken from "Starting from Paumanok" in *Leaves of Grass*, and the song "A Ghoath Andeas!" on page 82 is from *Songs of the Irish* by Donal O'Sullivan.

ISBN: 0-440-22961-8

RL: 6.1

Reprinted by arrangement with Alfred A. Knopf, a division of Random House, Inc.

Printed in the United States of America

February 2002

10 9 8 7 6 5 4 3 2 1

OPM

Becoming Mary Mehan

TWO NOVELS

A NOTE ON THE PRONUNCIATION OF GAELIC WORDS AND NAMES IN THE TEXT

The most important word to pronounce is the name "Mairhe," the Irish form of "Mary." The vowel sound is pronounced approximately as "oi," thus, "Moira," although the actual sound of the name is hard to describe in words. *Dia dhuit* is pronounced "jia-gwitch," *Badb* is pronounced "Bove," and *slainte* is pronounced "slawn-cha." The name of the legendary hero Finn mac Cumhail is pronounced "Finn Macool."

The Dreams of Mairhe Mehan

PROLOGUE

WERE THESE MY dreams? Were these then my brother's dreams?

Was I my dreams?

I'll tell you what happened to Mike in the night, of the three sounds of sorrow, of Lincoln's hornpipe, of my Da.

I was Mairhe Mehan, and these were my dreams. Or perhaps it may be they were my brother's.

Or perhaps they never were dreams at all. Their province is the edge of things, as it was mine: in the doorway, on the threshold, in the twilight, between one world and another.

So who can say if they happened or no? They're true enough, that I swear. They're woven tight and strong as any story is woven, thread following thread, the patterns emerging, the knots broken, the stitches dropped and reclaimed, the loose ends left or tied, the way we weave our own lives.

They are stories. I'll tell them.

MIKE IN THE NIGHT

1

TWO FEDERAL SOLDIERS stumbled out of a whorehouse on North Capitol Street, drunk as lords. One, a short sort with ginger whiskers, leaned over and began to puke in the gutter, and Mike, who was passing, began to laugh.

"Happy New Year to you," he said. He stamped through a puddle of muddy slush.

The one who could still stand stood still, and fixed Mike with an evil eye. "You damned Irish nigra. Get out of my way."

Mike bowed, and he knew the man would have at him, so he bulled forward, swinging his brickie bag to catch the soldier on the chin. All in a moment the man was on his back in the icy street.

Ginger stood up, stared at Mike, and then at his friend. "Boys!" he called over his shoulder.

The whorehouse door opened and a gust of infantry blew out with noise and whiskey fumes. Mike, ever a dancer, judged his card was too full and skipped away whistling, but the sounds of pursuit reached him and he began to run, down a dark alley, over a dung heap, vaulting a fence. A dog snarled out and slunk away and the wind sang in Mike's ears, and the light laugh rang out of him and ahead in the dark another noise began: glass breaking, a harlot shrieking, men laughing.

With unsteady breath and the grin of all devils, Mike pressed himself to the wall, and stole a view around the corner. Baker's boys, the Capital Police, were throwing bottles into the ashyard from the back door of another whorehouse. The smell of the liquor filled the cold air like the smoke of a battlefield, and a broad bawd screeched like a banshee and kicked men's shins.

Mike crept closer to the scene, well in the shadow, while the bottles burst like shells all around him. And when next the detective chucked a bottle over his shoulder, Mike sprang out and plucked it from the air and was gone again in the dark without breaking stride and the fellow looked back at the absence of smash.

Mike! Mike! The valorous fox, caparisoned horse, the dancer, the poet of deeds!

And so with a bottle he jigged his way back through Washington to Swampoodle, and there he found me, dreaming in my chair.

"Mairhe, girl, light us a fire, it's cold as the grave," he said, uncorking his bottle.

And I with my knees tucked up, and my black hair all down my back like a blanket, looked up at him with his glittering eyes. His throat moved as he swallowed.

"Don't let Da see what you've got," I told him.

I put aside the lace I was making, and stood and took his dinner from the shelf, and set it before him and stood and watched him eat. Mike attacked his meal like any wolf does. Between his bites and his parleys with the bottle, he told me of his day's work at the Capitol.

"And it was that cold the mortar hardly held, and the bricks like old kings' bones in your frozen hand, and the site boss was mad as a hornet for three men joined the Army last night and never came to work."

"Fools," I said.

Mike regarded me. "Fools how?"

"Fools to fight a war."

"Mairhe, girl, you're a girl."

"I know it, Michael Mehan. I've seen myself in the glass."

"And cannot have a political opinion in your head, so don't talk about things you don't know. The rebs—"

"The rebs?" came Da's voice.

He held himself upright in the doorway, and aimed one finger at Mike. "And why shouldn't the South break away? I ask you. Lincoln's no better than the English Crown, forcing itself and union onto Ireland."

Mike swung the bottle by the neck, his eyes on Da. "Ah, but now they say it's a war to free the slaves."

"Letting those blacks free will only drive down our wages," Da muttered, his eye following the bottle's arc.

"Whose wages?"

"I earn a wage!" Da roared. "I have been unable to work of late, is all!"

"Of late? I like that!" Mike shouted back, banging the bottle onto the table so hard that a gulp of whiskey pitched up through the neck and wet Mike's hand. "Late last summer, was it? You and your wild temper'd have us living in the street!"

"Don't *temper* me! Don't you *temper* me! No son of mine shall speak to me this way!"

"What'll you do, beat me? I'm not a child any longer, you're not stronger than me any longer!"

Da was white with rage. "In Ireland—"

"In *Ireland*? God help us!" Mike groaned. "What'd you bring us to America for, you crazy drunkard, if you love that country so much?"

And a thumping on the floor below us began, and a dog barked at the yelling and someone scolded in Gaelic. On the other side of the wall, someone coughed and cursed.

"Mike!" I stepped before him, and placed my hand over his eyes. I could feel them moving beneath my hand, could feel his angry breathing on my hand, and I whispered, "Go out."

He moved away from me, and headed for the door, but as Da took a step toward the bottle, Mike reached back and plucked it away. Da stood reaching for the empty air, and Mike was gone.

"Oh, my girl," Da said, easing slowly into a chair. His hands shook. "I've come a most unexpectedly long way down. Back in Sligo the Mehans were respectable, but then the Hunger came and who could stop it, then?"

"I know, Da." I straightened his coat, and he leaned back his head, his gray hair spilling over his collar like the strings of a broken harp. "I know."

"And where has your brother gone?"

I closed my eyes, and could see him in the street, clapping hands with his friends, linking arms with them as they began to march.

I dreamed my brother was gone for a soldier. When I cried out, Da shifted in his chair.

"What is it, then?" he asked.

I drew my coat about my shoulders. "Nothing, Da," I said. "Go to sleep."

"And where are you off to, girl, at this time of the night?"

I stopped at the door. "To work, Da. Remember? This is when I go to work."

"Oh. Yes," he said. "Yes." And subsided into himself with his chin on his chest and his dream was written plain on his face: Take me home. Take me back to my own country.

I slipped out the door. Down the dark stairs, feeling my way in the dark, I heard the wants of people living around us: more food, a better job, someone to love me, make my son good, take this cough from me. And try as I might, those were all plain to my ear, though I turned up the collar of my coat and stumbled in my haste.

Yet there at the doorway to the street did I pause, and look out at Swampoodle, where all those wants were multiplied a thousand thousand times. I didn't like to go out into them. But I went.

And what did I do but step in the mud the moment I gained the street? Mud, and frozen too, was everywhere in Swampoodle. Why else such a dreary name? The Tiber Creek slouched through the neighborhood like a dirty drunk who won't leave, and sighed into our Swampoodle its damp, unlovely breath. Down the street I could see the lights from St. Aloysius making a halo around the church in the mist. An ambulance wagon was stuck in a muddy rut outside the door. The two drivers were swearing at the mules, which you might think were named Jesus and Mary from the way the men exhorted them.

I turned my back on the soldiers, and headed for the Shinny, cracking the ice in the ruts as I went in my muddy shoes.

The Shinny, now, what was it named for? For the broken shinbone of the old man, Dooley, who was host of the establishment? Or for the shindigs and shenanigans of the Irish boyos who leaned their elbows against the bar? Or for the pole on the roof many a man tried to shinny up to win a bottle of whiskey, and from which many a man had fallen? Who cared? said I whenever anyone asked. For to me the Shinny meant work, and that was all, and I didn't waste my dreams on it. I'd seen it at its best and worst, and there wasn't much difference between them.

Red-faced Mrs. Dooley was planted before the

stove when I went in the back door. The frying pan before her hissed with sausage and peeled praties, and she poked at them with a fork. There was a roar of noise from the front of the house. New Year's Eve at the Shinny, and there must have been every able-bodied man in Swampoodle there.

"Mairhe, you're late."

"Sorry. Is my brother here?"

"Isn't he always?" Mrs. Dooley jabbed the sausages again. "Go on with you."

I put on an apron and went out into the saloon. Thick with smoke it was, and loud with the shouts of men and the crack of one man after the other pounding his glass down on the bar. Volleys of opinion shot back and forth through the fray, and a man howled out loud in the corner. A sign above the counter read, "No Soldiers Served." I ducked around behind the bar where Dooley was, and saw my brother Mike at home at the center of his fellows—O'Callahan, the O'Neill brothers, Milky Wesley with his bloody terrier, Snatcher, the scourge of Swampoodle's rats, nipping heels and ankles and sniffing among the sawdust of the floor.

"Start pulling," Dooley said for hello.

I grabbed a glass and held it below the tap, and pulled it full of ale.

Mike caught my eye and winked, and raised his glass to me. A pack of dog-eared cards was spread across the bar before him. I could see he was in the middle of a fine performance.

"It came to me today," he was saying. "Aren't there fifty-two cards to a deck? And fifty-two weeks to a year?"

A man beside him nodded the wise nod of a man in his cups. "To be sure. To be sure."

"And so it reasons, therefore, that each card must signify a week of the year." Mike held up the queen of hearts. What a grin he had. "This lovely lady, now. She's the first week of summer."

"Go on with you, Mike." Another man stirred the cards with a dirty finger and plucked one out. "Here, what's the week for the two of clubs?"

"Second week of the year," Mike answered at once. "A lowly week, and a dark one, and a long way to go."

Dooley put his meaty elbows on the bar. "And the first week?"

"The first week?" Mike looked around. They loved him. He had drawn almost every man in the place. "Tomorrow begins the first week of January. It looks to the future, and has a bellyful of good plans and ambitions, but it's cold, boys. Very cold. Call it the ten of diamonds."

"More like the jack of spades, this year," called a man in the rear. "Taking Emancipation into the argument."

Someone else shushed him. "Be a good Christian, man. Where's your charity?"

Mike turned, eyes sparkling. "Jack of spades? That's what you say, Dick Finn?"

Fair-haired Finn moved forward into the fray. "I do. Them blacks'll take our jobs once they're free, every man jack of 'em, and it's a black day when that happens. Let 'em stay slaves is what I say."

"Get out, Finn, you drunken eejit! You can't see sense when it spits in your ear," cried Leary. "You've mistook the entire argument for this war!"

"I'm not drunk, Leary," Finn shot back. "I'm the soberest man here, I tell you."

"The black man is the Irishman's companion in the general disregard of the nation! They'll have *us* slaves next if we don't emancipate our African brothers!"

"Brothers my eye!"

Some shouted against Leary, and some shouted against Finn, and others shouted just to be making noise. Snatcher set to barking for the sport of it all. I sent Mike a look. He'd started it to make trouble, I did not doubt. It may be he hadn't guessed what trouble he'd start, but he knew he'd rouse a fight and he delighted in it. He turned away from the yelling and barking and leaned across the bar to me.

"How's about a glass while Dooley's popping his

buttons?" Mike said, pushing his foam-ringed glass to me.

I pulled a glass for him. "Do you take a side in this argument?" I asked.

"Me take a side, Mairhe? Me?" He swallowed half his ale and belched discreetly into his hand. "I'm as fair and impartial as the day is long."

"Don't take a side," I warned my brother. "This war's none of our business."

"Now, my girl." Old Leary finger-pointed me straight. "It is indeed, for it is in our interest to test that a republic can survive such factioning and fractioning and come out whole. Else how can Ireland hope ever to make a republic of itself?"

"But the *Dublin News* is of the opinion that what was herebefore an unholy partnership is well disposed of." That was Mr. Lewes, who hooked his thumbs in his armpits and tucked in his chin. "And so leave it alone, let the South go, but don't fight for the slave states. Good riddance to them, let the republic restore itself without them."

"Here's the way of it," squint-eyed John O'Callahan was saying. He pounded on the bar to be heard. "This war's a training for us Fenians, and when we're practiced in the art of it, we're off to Ireland to rout the English. Those Irish sons who've no wish to go home and free the country are no Irish sons atall."

"Hear, hear!"

"And so it makes no difference to the Fenians which side you take, so long as you learn the trade of war?" Mike asked.

O'Callahan weaved a bit from side to side. He squinted harder at Mike. "What's that?"

"Which side do you take?" Mike asked.

"Whichever side'll have him!" Dooley said with a laugh. "And won't they be fighting to get such a specimen as our O'Callahan? Come, boys, it's New Year's Eve. Let's give politics a holiday."

The men broke up at that, and in the far corner two men with fiddles began scratching a tune. Milky caught up Snatcher in his arms and danced with him to the delight of the crowd, while the little ratter cocked his head one way and the other like a comical tiny man. Mike rested his cheek on his hand and smiled at me. He looked sleepy.

"Why do you do it, Mike?" I asked.

"What is it I do, sister darling?"

"Make trouble. Stir up fights. You're such an enemy to peacefulness and quiet."

"Fighting's my nature, sweet Mairhe. A man must fight."

I glared at him. "Don't come at me with that story. Only the foolish fight."

He smiled again, and rubbed his cheek against his hand like a tired hound. "You don't under—"

"I don't understand, I know, you've told me often enough," I broke in. "I understand you love to throw things into the air to see if they'll fall and smash, and I don't want you going off to try the war just to see the pieces break. It's none of our business. It's their fight, not ours."

"Why's that, Mairhe? Altogether Irish, are you? Pining for the dear old sod?"

"Not that."

"Ah, go home, little colleen. Go on with you. Take Da and go home. This is America. We want only the tryers and strivers here." He waved me away. "Off with the Fenians you go, back to the land of the forlorn and the faint hope."

There was a knot in me I thought might break, he pulled it so hard. "I'm not like Da. And I'm no Fenian. I've no plan to go back."

"Then you're American, is that right?"

I couldn't answer that. I had the excuse of needing to work, and I pulled glasses full of ale as rapidly as Dooley set them before me. Mike stayed where he was, for once out of the fray, and made circles on the bar with his finger.

The look of him made me want to weep, suddenly. "Mike, what's the trouble?" I asked.

He made to smile, but instead he drew his breath on a sigh. "Mairhe, I'm tired."

"So're we all, Mike."

"Ah, but you sleep when you're tired. I don't sleep. I close my eyes, but it's nothing but darkness and fearful dreams tearing at my soul. I lift a plate of food, only to see it break into pieces in my hand. I try to build, but the bricks crumble as I lift them, stairs crack so I can't go up, I walk down a street looking for home, but the house turns to dust before my weeping eyes."

I touched his hand. "It's only dreams, Mike."

"I hate them. I hate the night, for that's when they come to me." The black hair fell across his eyes. He turned upon the crowded room, with the tramp of the men stamping with the music, the fiddlers poking the smoke with their bows, the devilish small dog snapping in circles and running at shadows. "And it's always the night with me," Mike said in a low, low voice. "And I'll never see a dawn."

2

IN THE NIGHT I dreamed I was a little girl with my Da, and we were going back to Ireland. We stood at the prow of a ship that leaped forward like any horse does, over the sea and its creaming waves, into the wind that smelled of grass. Da stood straight and tall, and he laughed down at me, his teeth white, his black hair streaming like a horse's mane.

"Look what I've got for you, my girl," he said, and drew from his pocket a doll of mine that had been broken, its leg snapped from its body by brother Mike. "It's whole again," he said.

"You've fixed it for me, Da?"

"And look. This and this," he went on, and pulled from all his pockets, and from the case that appeared at his side, all the broken things of my childhood: toys, and childish creations of wood and straw, and ripped clothes and tangled lace and a wounded bird that flew out from Da's hand and ahead of the ship, singing. "And this and this and this," Da kept saying as one after the other came new and whole.

And he laughed, and he was whole himself, and unbroken.

3

I WAS MAIRHE Mehan, and the truest thing I knew was I loved my brother, and that his heart was a good heart.

How could he have such a dream, then, when

Emancipation came with the first day of 1863, and some Irishmen went hunting for a black man to hurt?

January 1: another cold day, and the brickies at the U.S. Capitol were arguing with the Italian masons who did the lovely work of stone and sculpture on the new fine dome. The brickies wished to work on the lee side of the building, and the masons wouldn't have them there, and the whole thing fell into argument and strife, for who wished to work on a day that should be a holiday? And down came the winter night so fast there was no more working anyway.

And off Mike went with the O'Neill boys, Jack and Dan, into the streets, where the caissons and the carts of artillery and the hospital wagons with their loads of broken soldiers had rutted the mud into frozen ridges. Pennsylvania Avenue was a mire, pitted and littered as a battleground.

"It's criminal," Jack said, his green eyes small with hate. "They've brought over those Italians and called them artisans. The fools don't even speak a language God can understand."

Mike had his head down against the wind, for he was tired, and the cold was aching him. The skin of his knuckles was broken and red, skinned where he'd fumbled the bricks in the clumsiness of cold. "Such a grand Capitol the government must have," he muttered. "A monument to the strength of my arm is what that building is."

"Nor are we welcome in it." Jack spit on the ground.

Dan made no comment. His was a dull mind, as all his fellows knew, and neither Mike nor his brother expected him to give an opinion. Dan strode through the wind, paying it no heed. His back was broad, and to Mike, who walked behind him, it looked like a stable door.

Government buildings at the side of the avenue echoed the sounding of sentries' march. Cannons flanked this building and that, announcing the capital's fear of Lee. The general and his rebs were only over the river, skipping around Virginia like boys on a lark, while in winter camp at Falmouth the Union boys in the Army of the Potomac squatted in their shanties and cursed the mealworms out of their bread. New Year's Day and nobody was getting any joy of it, least of all Mike. Alongside Pennsylvania Avenue, the City Canal gave off a stink of garbage and dead cat.

The ground beneath their feet trembled and rumbled with the movement of distant wagons, giving its itch and its restless ache up into the Irishmen that walked the road. Mike felt it in himself, and saw it in the flex and stretch of Jack's hands, and in Dan's immovable back.

"Let's off to the President's House," Mike said with a wave, for up ahead all the distant length of the avenue was the shining white hideout of the leader of the Republic.

"I hate that Lincoln," said Jack.

"Jack hates ever'one," spoke Dan. And he laughed the sort of laugh a bull might make if it took it in its head to be mean.

"Lincoln's all right," Mike declared. "But he dresses like a bloody undertaker. Come on."

He hunched his shoulders against the cold. The wind blew cinders into his eyes as he pressed onward, and blew the black dust from a charcoal seller's wagon.

So Jack with his scowl and Dan with his milk-faced foolish frown followed after, plodding through the grit-blowing dark. And then they must share the avenue with the smart carriages and equipages pulled by polished horses with arched necks. The stream of traffic grew stronger and louder, and the current rolled on toward the President's House behind its oval of lawn trod bare by drilling soldiers and pastured beef. The house shot light through every window. The visiting throng pressed up the stairs as the leavers retreated. Inside, somewhere, a great gloomy man in black shook hands as he had done all day for the New

Year's Reception, commander in chief of a noisy review to which all comers were welcome.

The Irish boys stood on the hard bare lawn where the carriages jostled for space, and blew into their hands. Mike danced from foot to foot, looking up at the white columns and the crowded steps and the pouring-out light, looking at the house where a poor farm boy was the President. "Go in, shall we? Let's do, they can't turn us out from a public reception. And it'd be fair warmer inside, I know that."

Dan stood where he was, planted like a stump. A driver shouted to him to move, but Dan never listened.

"Go on!" The driver yelled again. "Give way!"

The horses shied and shook their heads, unwilling to pass too close by Dan, looming statue that he was.

"Give way, man!"

"Oh, go shag yerself!" Jack shouted, all provoked.

"Damned Irish!" came the driver back. He cracked his buggy whip in the air. "Give way, you stupid Irish bull!"

Dan turned at last to look up at the man. Then he looked at Jack. Jack nodded.

Mike clapped his hands in Jack's face. "In!

We're going in, Jack! Let's tell Lincoln what an old crow he is."

When nobody moved, the driver at last gave up in disgust and backed his roll-eyed horses. Jack was glaring up at the steps of the President's House. "I hate Lincoln," he said quietly. "I hate the Italians. I hate the Americans. And mostly I hate them."

And Mike looked where Jack was looking, and saw a black man coming down the steps, a tall hat on his head, pulling white gloves onto his hands. Laughing he was, and giving a good-night to a comrade at his side, and turning up the collar of his heavy cloth coat. Then he parted from his friend, and made his way past the military guards and the clusters of muffed and hatted ladies stepping into carriages, and so to the street. Jack took off after him, hands dug deep in his pockets. Dan followed dumbly behind his bad brother.

Mike stood where he was, in the shadow of a pillar, and then chased after his friends. None of them spoke, for the night was cold and their purpose was a stealthy one. Up ahead, the man in the tall hat walked with a joyous stride, swinging a cane, humming with gladness on this day of Emancipation, all unaware of the men following him in the dark. Voices fell away behind them. The street was empty but for them.

"Jack, let's find us a saloon," Mike said. He

snapped a bare twig from a branch that overhung the sidewalk. "Let's us go to Foggy Bottom."

"Shut up."

The man ahead seemed to hesitate, and then walked on. Jack stopped, and Dan stopped, and Mike also. The man turned around. He stood straight.

"Who is it?"

Nor Mike, nor Jack, nor Dan spoke. They were all in the night.

"I am Dr. Mason," the man said. "Do you have business with me?"

Jack stepped forward where a light fell onto him. "You and your kind," he made in answer.

"Come away," Mike said.

Jack heeded him not at all, and Dan stepped forward with his brother. Mike saw the doctor's shoulders sag with the heaviness of it all.

"I am not carrying money," the doctor said. "Do not accost me. There's nothing to gain."

Jack and Dan went forward with no more words. Mike saw the lie of the land and liked it not at all, and he turned and slipped back into the shadows and was gone. He ran into the dark, cutting north toward Swampoodle, and the night chasing him all the way.

4

DA WAS IN fine fettle an evening or so after the New Year. He rose from an afternoon's sleep with a mind for mending.

"I've a good feeling about tomorrow," he said as he sat at the table across from me. "Give us some tea, daughter."

"Kettle's just on. It'll be a minute." I was working at some lace before heading for the Shinny. Ten cents a yard it fetched, but hard on the fingers were those ten cents.

Da sat and watched me, and the kettle ticked and muttered on the stove behind me. Da drummed his fingers on the table. I looked from below my lashes, at his drumming fingers. So scarred and bent they were, so worn and the nails so cracked and yellow.

"I believe tomorrow is a day I'll find work."

I stopped in my work, then went on, my fingers never halting. I chose not to look at him. "Ah, is that right, Da?"

"Yes. I do believe so. A man should bestir himself at the start of a new year. All things are possible to a man who only strives."

"That's sure."

"And I know, my girl, that you've had a worry for

me. But those jobs I had were the wrong jobs, and the bosses against me, every man of them. I'll find a job I can stick with. Something worthy of a Mehan. Worthy."

"I know it, Da."

"That's right. I'll show them. I'll show them all what an Irishman can do."

I ducked my head lower over my work. "Yes, Da."

"Ah, Mairhe. Did I ever tell you of what happened to me at Sligo Fair, when as a young man, I was considered the finest fighter in Connacht?"

The kettle fussed, and the distant shouts of an argument and laughter downstairs were like the shouts of farmers at market fair, of sheep and kine crying on the road to auction. I knew this story. Of Matthew Mehan, handsome fellow, kicking the straw from his way and stooping under the ropes to meet the challenger, while the assembled folk laughed and clapped and laid their wagers, and a cool breeze off the ocean tossed the fine dark hair into Matthew's eyes. And behind all heads a sky so blue, and the clambering hills so mossed with green.

Da scraped his chair back, and stretched out his hands to clasp behind his neck. For a few moments we were quiet. I wished I might only work on my lace; my fingers knew the knots to make, my bobbin knew what holes to dance through. The slender threads clung to one another and grew slowly forward like lichen across a gray stone.

Da cleared his throat. His faded eyes sought mine with a plea.

"Yes, tell me about it, Da," I said at last.

He sighed, happy, and leaned back for storytelling. "It starts long ago in the time of Turloch O'Connor, and him so brave. Such a wild spalpeen of a lad, but the King of Connacht nonetheless, and took the O'Connors into war against the English at the Battle of Athenry."

"Yes, Da."

"And so with clash of halberd and pike, and the archers making a rain of arrows, and the ground thick with heart's blood. And in the midst of it all, one Brian Mehan of the Mehans saw his eldest son gored fornent his very eyes, in the hesitation of his heart. And from that day, Mehan swore to raise up his sons to be fighters who never hesitate, and never lose.

"In 1316 that was, but even so it was that as a lad, I too was raised to fight. And I used my fists against all comers in the ring. Every fair and market that cared to put up a purse saw me there, ready to fight. Never did I fail to win a bout, my girl. Never."

"No, Da," I murmured, my eyes on my lace. "No, sure you didn't."

"And it was there at Sligo Fair that I first saw

your mother, laughing and colloguing with her friends over a table of brass candlesticks. *Mavrone!* What a darling she was."

The kettle was chattering on the stove. I turned away from Da to stop him from speaking. Who can hear the same dream over and over without her heart breaking? I poured water into our jug pot, onto the old tea leaves that still sulked there, and let the steam bathe my cheeks.

Da was shaking his head and smiling. "No, no. A Mehan never loses. Fighters always. We pick our fights, and we never turn aside. True Irishmen. True to Ireland."

A silence came between us, and I dared not look into his eyes. Where was Mike? we neither of us asked. What fight was he fighting now? Where was he in the darkness of this night?

I sat down again with my lace, and measured my progress against my arm. Five cents. A few handspans of white web. Not much to cling to, was it?

And then in came Mike, and pulled out a chair while we sat without words to watch him, and he crossed his arms before him.

"I've signed papers and joined the Federals," said he. "I'll be leaving in a month for Falmouth."

"Jesus, no," said Da. "You're an Irishman."

And the bobbin fell from my fingers, and the

stitches in the lace came all undone, raveling out from my senseless hands.

5

I DREAMED I was at the Capitol, where the 8th Massachusetts was quartered in the Rotunda. It was dark inside, and the lamps smoked to make my eyes sting. I went from officer to officer, soldier to soldier, asking who'd done this terrible thing to my life. One officer, seated at a table, held a map to the lamp's light. He tipped the map this way and that to the light and frowned, as though there were some will-o'-the-wisp feature engraved there that only showed from one angle, and that he could not see for more than a moment.

"Was it you?" I asked.

This officer in his blue and braid did not look up. He did not hear me. Above his head, the Rotunda dome echoed with coughs, and the stamp of boots, and the rattle of rifles stacked together. Someone was brushing boots with a *sh-sh, sh-sh*. The officer turned down the lamp and rose from the table. I followed, and we passed out through a doorway into a dim corridor, where senators leaned against the wall in weariness, showing one another their bills and urging support.

"My brother's job is working here. He's helping to build this Capitol for the government," I told the officer, tugging on his sleeve. "He's not to go to war. He's to stay here and build."

The officer walked on, his saber banging against his leg. And then, at the far end of the corridor where a door led into darkness, he turned, and he was Mike.

"You'll never change my mind," said he. "I won't ever be moved in this."

He smiled. And then he went through the doorway into the night, leaving me there alone on the other side.

MEETING MR. WHITMAN

1

THE NOONTIME SHINNY was loud in my ears. I was attempting to clear a basin of dirty plates from the tables when Mr. O'Callahan came in, waving a two-cent newspaper like a flag. I went on with my work as he began.

"Listen to this, now, lads!" O'Callahan called. "Queen Victoria has addressed the Parliament on the question of 'the hostilities in the North American States.' "

"What's she say then, the old cow?"

There was a roar of laughter at Lewes's remark.

O'Callahan straightened his paper with a snap and read in a high, quavering voice. " 'We have abstained from attempting to induce a cessation of the conflict between the contending parties,' says she. 'Because it has not yet seemed to Her Majesty— ' er, I should say 'My Majesty,' " O'Callahan corrected himself. He winked at me.

"Go on, John," Dooley called from the bar.

"To continue," O'Callahan said. " 'It has not yet seemed to Her Majesty that any such overtures could be attended with a probability of success.' "

I hitched the full basin up onto my hip. "That's wisdom."

"Oho!" O'Callahan looked around at his friends, eyes wide, and then returned to me. "How's that now, Miss Mairhe Mehan? How do you come by such an understanding and sympathy with Queen Factoria?"

"Nothing will stop men from fighting one another if they've made up their minds to it," I said. "What's the good of reasoned arguments? I'm having no part of it, myself. Excuse me." And so I pushed by the men and into the kitchen.

And there, Mrs. Dooley stood as ever at her hissing stove.

"Give over, missus," said I. "I'll take a turn pushing the praties around if you like."

"Oh, Mairhe, good girl." Mrs. Dooley sat heavily down in her chair by the door, and fanned her hot face with her apron. "Those sausages are for

Mr. Finn, now. He likes 'em cooked dry through and through."

And so down I set the dishes with a thump, and took up the fork. In truth I liked it better in the kitchen, where the voices didn't shout so. I frowned down in the pan, poking the sausages and the praties, and glad to be out of the yelling in front.

"And how's your Da?" Mrs. Dooley asked, catching her breath in a gulp. "He doesn't come around anymore."

"No, missus, he's not feeling much his usual self and likes to bide at home."

"Ah, for shame. We've forgiven him these many months for breaking our door when he lost his last job, Mairhe, tell him that. He needn't be shy to come back."

"He's only feeling low," I said, the shame of it in my own face.

Mrs. Dooley stretched her legs before her and sighed. "Such a pity. He was ever a handsome man, Matthew Mehan. I call to mind the night he first came in here, so big, with that fine silver hair wild about his head and a fine beard and his blue eyes all smiling."

I nodded, for that was the father I dreamed in my dreams. A strider and a striver, and free with gesture and laughter both.

And then the door opened, and such a man walked in with a buffet of noise from the front of the house. Tall, and broad about the shoulders and shod in polished boots. This was the man my father was once.

"Mrs. Dooley?"

Mrs. Dooley and I only stared at the man conjured by our conversation. Before me on the stove a sausage popped and hissed. The man closed the door and looked at us.

"Mrs. Dooley?" he asked again.

"Yes, oh, to be sure," the woman replied, struggling to rise and fussing her apron. "What is it you're wanting, mister?"

He waved toward the door behind him. "Mr. Dooley says you know one Mrs. Pyle?"

"Kitty Pyle?"

"Kitty Pyle, yes. I have a charge to bring her the effects of her soldier grandson, who just last night died in the hospital. He said he had kin here in Washington City, and begged me bring his poor things to her."

Mrs. Dooley was all on guard in a moment. She eyed the man up and down. He wore no uniform nor insign.

"You're an army doctor, then?"

"No, I only sit with the boys, and read to them and do their small errands and write their letters.

See, I've written what address he knew—" And the man took from his pocket a sheaf of paper folded together and stitched with rough string on one side to make a book no larger than his hand. His broad thumb flipped the pages. "Mrs. Kitty Pyle, Swampoodle. It's all he knew. I can't make my way in this neighborhood."

Mrs. Dooley worked her lips in grave thought. She turned my way. "You take him, Mairhe. Mrs. Pyle lives round by Haney's."

The big man with the wild white hair looked from her to me and back again, his eyes wide and waiting.

I took my coat from its nail. "Follow me, mister." And went out the back door into the alley.

"Moira, is it? Myra?"

"Mairhe, yes," I replied, skirting empty crates, leading the way. Above the alley, a strip of high blue sky showed cold.

"I've only been in Washington since December. My brother was wounded at Fredericksburg and I came down to nurse him. Can't say I know my way around the whole city, yet. I've walked a good bit of it, but not Swampoodle."

"No reason to."

"I don't know," he said, stopping to gaze down a side street. "Any place with as fine a name as Swampoodle must have plenty to recommend it."

"I wouldn't recommend it, myself."

Our way led up the miry street to Cabbage Alley. Somewhere in the distance was a crack of gunfire from soldiers drilling, and the street was crowded with wagon traffic, and oxen complaining. I trod through the mud with the white-haired man lingering and looking along behind me.

He walked quiet and quick for a big man, and considered all around him with a curious eye. I watched him looking at the crowded window of a pawn shop, where sat a dainty harp in a copper cook pot. He smiled happily, and caught my eye.

"Music makes an excellent meal. I've dined on it many times and never felt hungry."

"I wonder how you came to be so big, then," I replied.

He put his head back and laughed. "I always eat a big breakfast. Lead on, Miss Mairhe."

And so we went along, skirting the worst of the puddles and the horse dung, and came abreast of St. Aloysius. Orderlies were unloading a wagonload of bread, lifting the baskets high and picking their way across the mud. My charge paused and looked up at the bold clock tower.

"Your church?" he asked.

"It's a hospital, now," I replied. "I don't go in anymore."

We walked on past it. I did not look. Ambulance

wagons waited around the corner at another door. I kept my eyes down, and kept a sharp watch for puddles. From the church-turned-hospital came the smell of chloroform, and blood, and men weeping.

"Why not?"

I glanced his way. His breath fogged from his lips.

"Why not what?" I asked him.

He halted, and waved back at St. Aloysius. "Why don't you go in? It's still a house of worship, if you choose to worship in a house."

"It's a house of fighters in pain. I won't worship there."

I clutched my coat tight around me. The cold was stealing up through the soles of my boots. My cheeks stung. The man didn't move.

"Sir. Mrs. Pyle is this way."

He still didn't move, but looked at me from below his brushy brows. "To my way of thinking, it's much holier now for the pain those fighters feel."

The stillness between us was broken by a scream from inside the church. I turned away and stumbled to be going, catching myself against the wall of a building as I went. "Not to my way of thinking. If you'll just follow me, sir."

"My name is Walt, Mairhe."

"This way, Mr. Walt."

He trudged along through the mud beside me. "They're good boys, all of them."

"Who's that, Mr. Walt?"

"The soldiers. You should go in sometime and visit with them. They're so lonely, you could do such good just to say hello."

I stopped by Haney's smithy.

"Sir, I will not go into the hospital. You've no call to scold and upbraid me this way."

He raised his eyebrows. "That's a strong reaction."

I looked away. "Mrs. Pyle is just in that house, through there," I said, pointing at the end of an alley.

Mr. Walt was a big reproachful bear beside me, chin sunk on his chest, and arms folded. His cheeks were red with the frost, and the rims of his ears. I wanted to push him down the alley. I wanted him to go away.

"Thank you for bringing me here, Mairhe. Mrs. Pyle's grandson was a good boy. He was brave before he died. He wanted his sister."

I breathed hard. "I am sorry for it."

He moved down the alley. In the distance, there was another round of gunfire.

I ran back to the Shinny by the long way around, so I wouldn't see the hospital again, and when I burst in through the kitchen door, Mrs. Dooley gave me the wide eye.

"What's gotten into you? You look that scared, I swear you're white as a pratie."

Carefully, carefully, I shut the door behind me, shut out the sounds of the war that were out there, everywhere. I wouldn't take a part in it, not for anything would I aid and succor the men who were breaking each other to bits. Mike wanted to break the best thing of all, now, and that was himself, and I hated him for it.

"Didn't try an impertinence with you, did he? That man?"

"No, missus." I blew on my hands to warm them, and rubbed them together over the stove.

Mrs. Dooley lifted a burner and jabbed her poker down in the fire, and the flames leaped up with a shower of sparks. In a moment was a dream before my eyes of men sitting around a fire, hunched in their oilcloth capes, their blue caps pushed low on their brows and a pot of coffee hissing and spitting into the embers.

"I'd like to find my brother, if you won't need me for a bit."

"Go on. Mind you don't stay away too long."

And so I left the Shinny again.

That was the first time that I met Mr. Whitman. I was soon to meet him again, though it was long before I'd know who and what he was to me. Seldom do we see through the shadows in our dreams when first we awake in the morning.

2

MIKE WAS AT the Capitol. The day was sore and bitter, and the brickies were compelled to do heavy labor, as the mortar wouldn't hold. He and the O'Neill boys were working in the shadow of the new dome, which rose like a skeleton above them.

Tall was the building, and stretching its wings out on either side to gather us all in its big embrace. The dome was like the sketch of an eagle's egg, waiting to be hatched, and the scaffolding holding it up like the twigs and sticks of a giant nest. Laborers were everywhere, nursing the thing to term. I could hold my hand before my face and block entirely the shape of that dome, yet between my fingers was a glimpse and another glimpse—it was a sight not to be blocked.

And oh, what an urgent and impatient Republic it was, that filled its Capitol to overflowing before the building was even complete. Senators and lawyerly men and soldiers and masons milled about the place like ants of an anthill, and the great congressional house built itself piece by piece into the blue air, as though the men who swarmed about it were transforming themselves into bricks and iron and stone to give the place shape.

On the grounds, a regiment was drilling, marching in file as a sergeant barked and brayed. I saw Dan punch Mike in the shoulder and laugh. Then did Mike catch sight of me, and ran to join me where I stood at the edge of things, my hand still lifted to the building.

"*Dia dhuit*," he said, and made me a bow. Jesus be with you.

"Don't mock me with your Irish hellos," I said.

"They say there's a rare little man at the President's House."

I laughed at his suddenness and quicksilver changing, and took his hands in mine to chafe them warm. "I always heard he was a great tall man."

"No, girl, today General Tom Thumb is to visit the President. Let's see if we can't spy him out." He danced me around.

"Mike, what are you about? Haven't you a job to do?"

He winked over at the shadows of the dome where Jack and Dan toiled. "The foreman can shag himself. I'll be joining my regiment in two weeks, so the job can go to blazes."

I had to laugh, but wouldn't let him drag me

along yet. "But you might change your mind and give up that idea, and so you'll need to keep your job."

"No. No. A thousand thousand times no, Mairhe, enough with your coaxings and claimings. Come along with you now. And for the matter of that," he added, cocking his head and fixing me with his grin, "what of your own job?"

"The Shinny can bide without me for a bit. How many times does an Irish girl get to see a tiny, tiny man? For all our own men are such giants and heroes in our eyes."

"Saucy harlot you are."

And so we went smiling up the avenue, all the while Mike telling me what he'd heard about the little man from Mr. Phineas T. Barnum's cavalcade of wonders, and how the little general had married his little lady love, and they were the tiniest pair and could go sailing in a teacup and paddle themselves about with silver spoons, and how Willard's Hotel was drawing the crowds to see the two wee grandees take their coffee of a morning.

"But we'll catch sight of them going in to see the old black crow," Mike said, and giving a wide smile to a matron as we passed.

"You've got a liking to look at the President's House," I said to him.

"Perhaps I do."

"Perhaps you think you'll live in it yourself one day."

"Ha, that an Irishman should do that," Mike laughed. "We're good for soldiers, not commanders."

I frowned. "Never say so."

A sparrow flicked into the street and away, and I followed it with my eyes to see a column of marching soldiers. My stomach turned. I'd suddenly the wildest wish to see General Tom Thumb and his miniature bride, all cheer and marvel. I'd a wild wish to get away from the sight of soldiers.

And so we joined a crowd standing outside the white mansion, and there was laughing and jokes, and a fat man with a voice from Boston read from a newspaper about the wedding ceremony (Mr. Barnum presiding), and there were many guesses how far up Lincoln's longshanks leg the general would stand, or what number of chairs and tables he'd have to climb to look Lincoln in the eye. And didn't Mike have to join in with the guessing and joking, and didn't he soon have all of a crowd around himself watching him and listening to him, rogue that he was.

And the fat man's fat wife, bundled in a black bonnet, screeched with jolly laughter and patted her cheek. "Don't say so!" she begged with tears standing on her lashes. "Don't say so!" Beside her, a man with a wide Ohio accent and sandy side whiskers offered his lunch around—a dented pail of tawny biscuits—and three solemn girls as alike as three new potatoes in their russet hats and capes said in chorus, "Where's General Thumb, for we've hemmed tiny hankies for him!" The weather was fine and fair and frosty, and the spirit of holiday warmed the crowd in their boots and their scarves. I saw two lovers kiss, and a woman cradle her pink babe at her shoulder. And so Mike went on, composing a very ballad of General Thumb as he stood there, and I, laughing with the rest of them, stepped back to the edge of the crowd and saw again the same white-haired man so like my father walking past, and he saw me.

"Well, Mairhe, I didn't imagine to meet you again today or ever." Mr. Walt hailed me from the middle of the street and strode near. The living breath puffed from him like steam from a train as he came.

"My brother." I gestured toward Mike. "We came to see the midgets."

Mr. Walt's eyes widened. "Is that right? All these people are here to see General Thumb?"

He turned to regard the noisy crowd. The faces, all the faces, were bright with cold and with laughing. The Ohio man. The fat Boston man and his fat wife. The pink babe and the hanky girls. And my brother, at home amongst them all like their own darling son or brother. Mr. Walt smiled, and smoothed down his beard. "Beautiful, aren't they?"

"Sir?"

"All the population in their coats and mittens, joining on the street outside the President's House, meeting their fellows together. Talking and talking, like one body with many voices." Mr. Walt spread his arms wide. "The farmer, the mechanic, the fisherman, the country doctor and the city doctor, the young mother and the old mother, east west, north south . . . I like to come here, myself, and look at him," he added suddenly, rounding on me.

I was surprised. "Look at who? Tom Thumb?"

"Lincoln. I have rooms over on K Street nearby Lafayette Square, and so I like to think us neighbors."

"You might call on him at teatime, then," I suggested.

He smiled at me. "I might. He's a common man. But one of the uncommonest kind. Too busy for a clerk like me to pester him, though."

Mr. Walt beamed at me, and listened to the crowd, and I couldn't recall why he'd frightened me so. He was a goodly man.

"Mr. Walt—"

Smiling still, he nodded as though in answer to a question. Then he held out his hand and I shook it.

"I'm off to Armory Square hospital, on my regular rounds as a roving beside-the-bed sitter," he said to me. "There's a Brooklyn boy had his leg shot off. I know his family. I promised to take him an orange."

And he dug in his pocket and brought out an orange from the Carib, gleaming and bright and round in his callused hand. He tossed it up, and I followed it into the air with my gaze until it disappeared into the glary dazzle above us.

I blinked, and shielded my eyes. But Mr. Walt kept his hand out, and in a moment it fell into his palm again. Then there he went through the yawping, yammering, gift-giving American crowd, a big dreamy man with a sun in his hand.

3

ONCE UPON A time were twin brothers, dearer to their father than cream from a lovely cow, dearer than dew on a pasture, dearer than the curve of a baby's cheek. The father was king of a fair and wide domain, and much taken up with the wise management of it. Yet upon his death the succession had not been arranged, and so the two boys settled on ruling together.

But one had ideas for the sovereignty of this land that did not concur with the ideas of the other brother. Soon discussion led to argument, and a division of lands where one would hold sway over the other. It wasn't of course a plan that could work, and before much time had passed from the father's death, the country went to war on itself.

And what was the natural outcome of war but the death and destruction of all that the two brothers loved? Each brother in his camp asked his own oracles to name the one blow that would cripple the other army. And each oracle said: Kill your brother, murder his family, salt his wells.

So heartsore were they two that upon that instant they laid down their weapons, and sought one another and embraced one another, swearing never to make war again.

This was the way that peace came back to that domain: learning that the only route to victory was to crush his brother foe utterly was a road none wished to travel.

This, of course, is not a story about the United States of America.

Nor is it a story of Ireland.

4

I WAS IN the Shinny of a dark afternoon later in the month, working my lace and listening to Dooley tell us a battle tale of Finn mac Cumhail, and from down the bar came interjecting the reports of how Mr. and Mrs. Lincoln were marking the one-year anniversary of their son Willie's death, as read from the paper by Ditty O'Herlihy, and I wove it all together into my lace.

" '. . . is said to be spending the day in prayer . . .' "

". . . and the stones of the road calling out that here lay his son beneath them . . ."

" '. . . while the Secretary of War read dispatches in the next room . . .' "

". . . and the ax broke into pieces in the father's hand, and he tore the silver hair from his head at the death of his son . . ."

" '. . . but a parent's grief must give way to the urgency of the hour . . .' "

". . . and the warrior king broke his shield in four and threw the pieces to the points of the four winds . . ."

" '. . . and subordinate personal loss for the good of the country in this time of war and national loss . . .' "

". . . before losing his heart entirely and wandering the land all the rest of his days, calling on the name of his son . . ."

And just as this country and all our legends and heroes were falling to pieces, so was my own family. For in rushed our neighbor Maud Shea, pale as a banshee, screaming to me as she clutched the air.

"Mairhe! Your father! Such a fit this time! He's wrecking the place!"

"Jesus and Mary." I was out the door and running, and the population of the Shinny running behind me too, like the ragged hem of an old woman's dress, dragging along in the mud.

The light was fading into a weary winter twilight, and the dimming sky above the street was an easier road to follow than the dark path at my feet. The blood of my heart beat a stumble against my ears. Yet it wasn't loud enough to cover the sound of breaking and crashing that drew me around the corner to find a crowd outside our building, and see the crockery, clothes, and chairs come flying through the window above. At each missile the crowd would draw away, and then press in again to pick up and pick over the broken shards of my family's household. Above it all, blurry and far away, was the yelling of my Da.

I took the stairs with my throat tearing on each breath. Another crowd filled the stairwell and clustered on the landings: women stretching their shawls around bony shoulders, grimy children with round black eyes. The yelling came clearer as I dragged myself up.

"Take it! Take it for we'll not need it anymore!"

How could such a poor household as ours have enough to throw from a window for more than two minutes together? Yet there was Da when I went into the room, dragging the drawers from the dresser, and tipping them out into the street. My own silver-headed Da was throwing our lives to the four winds.

"My father!" cried I. "My father, no!"

He stumbled and turned around, and his face broke into a glad smile. The whites of his eyes were shot red. "Mairhe, daughter! I can use your help." And he went for the dresser again but I stood myself before it.

"What are you doing!"

"We're leaving, Mairhe," he said, catching his breath and looking pleased. "Gave up the rooms. And I'll never regret leaving this dirty hole, either," he added with a broad kingly gesture of disgust.

My ears were ringing. "My father, why did you give up the rooms? Where is it we'll live?"

"No, no, Mairhe. No, no." And he was shaking his head, and trying to get past me to pull out a drawer. "We're selling all this and going home to Connacht."

I stood my ground, and he squinted and tried to get by me but couldn't, and I thought I might cry, or vomit on the floor. The place looked like a land where a war's been, all things upended and disarrayed, every pitiful thing we owned burst from its rightful place and ruined. Mugs, plates, bowls lay in shards, clothes and cloths hung or lay about like the lifeless hulls of slain soldiers, coal was strewn about the floor like shrapnel.

Da gave up trying to get by me, and stood regarding his work with a critical eye. He nodded, and bent to pick up the leg of a broken chair. He walked with a ruined grace, a crippled boxer with no one to fight but himself.

"My father, we're not going home."

"We are."

Where the window was, the light was giving up and going away. In the corners of the room where the dark was, the edges of my life were blurring. Da stood where he was, hefting the broken chair leg in one hand, testing its weight like a war ax.

There was a noise behind me at the door. Dooley was there, and John O'Callahan, old friends both of my Da. Someone behind them held a lamp, and its light seeped in around their heads like something leaking from an old glass.

"Matthew."

Dooley came toward Da, kicking the broken things out of his way. I feared Da would strike at him with the stick, but Da only looked at his friend. Dooley took him by the arm, and led him out into the hall. O'Callahan stepped aside as they came, and walked in to me, nervously rolling his eyes this way and that at the spectacle of battle fought within the walls.

"Mairhe, they say he did give up the rooms, and they're already let," O'Callahan whispered. "Can't stay on here."

"Where's Dooley taking him?"

"To St. Aloysius, see if they'll take your father in on the parish," O'Callahan continued in the same awed whisper. He looked about in the dimness and whistled. "Sh'll I get my wife to help you take up your t'ings, Mairhe?"

I hung my head. I saw nothing to save. "No, thank you, Mr. O'Callahan. There's nothing here, now."

So I left the rooms and went feeling my way down the stairs like any old woman does who's seen the power of destruction let loose in her life. Dooley and my Da were just leaving the house through the curious crowds. I stopped in the doorway to watch them, and then followed them out and down the street toward St. Aloysius.

As we neared the church, its strong lights threw a gleam around my Da's white head, and around Dooley like a brawny ambulance man propping him up. And forward they two went to the side door of the church. I saw the door open, and the robed figure of the chaplain, and Dooley's head moving as he spoke.

And then was my Da welcomed in, and he went in with the rest of the wounded and crippled soldiers and the door closed behind him. I could not move from where I was, though Dooley looked back at me and then came my way.

"Come on, girl, you'll stay at the Shinny. Mrs. Dooley loves you like a daughter anyway. You'll come see your Da tomorrow."

That I doubted, though I didn't speak my doubt to Dooley.

5

AND WHERE WAS Mike for all of this? Croosheening in the ear of a pretty girl he met outside Willard's Hotel, when he was hanging about to see the officers and learn a military swagger. He was to go to Falmouth in the morning, and damned if he wouldn't spend his last night as a free man spinning some kind of yarn for a pair of fair blue eyes.

"Say you'll walk with me along the river," he begged. "Yours may be the last sweet face I take to war with me."

This Ellie Anderson showed him her dimples. "Are you really joining your regiment tomorrow?"

"I am." Mike showed the way toward the Potomac, and they fell into step. He knew when to speak, and when not to. He gazed ahead, into the winter sunset, a look of tragedy on his face.

"I think you're awful brave," Ellie said. "Aren't you scared of going into the war?"

Mike shrugged a no. "I come from a long line of soldiers, Ellie. My father and grandfather and so back and back fought beside all the great American patriots. We're one of the oldest soldiering families in the land. A Mehan doesn't know fear."

"But I thought you were an Irish boy!"

"Did you?" Mike guided her around a puddle and they stood by the Chain Bridge.

Her eyes were downcast. She feared she had insulted him. "Your accent. You sound like an Irish boy."

"The accent lingers in the family," Mike told her with a laugh. "And I've lately spent time among the poor of Swampoodle, learning their ways and gaining the trust of those I will lead. I suppose it brings out the Irish in my voice."

They stood at the bank of the black river by the heavily guarded bridge. A cold wind pressed against them. Ellie shivered, and drew her coat closer, and drew nearer Mike, who made his own warmth.

"Your family must be proud," she said.

"I only do my duty." Mike waved one hand to take in the river and the opposite shore. "Our country. Father never ceases to speak of it. It is his most ardent wish that I defend it."

Ellie looked at him. The setting sun put gold on his cheeks. No doubt she thought he was a marvel.

"And your mother? Doesn't she mind awfully?"

"She died— no," he added when Ellie cried out. "It was long ago, in a smallpox epidemic. She left our fine house and went among the people of Swampoodle who were suffering so, and she nursed and cared for them, never giving a thought to her own health and strength."

"Ah." A sigh passed Ellie's red lips. "Your whole family then is a family of brave heroes. And so much on behalf of the poor Irish."

Mike stooped to pick up a rock, and he chucked it at a stick that went floating past. "They're much despised, the poor Irish. I see them sometimes at work on the Capitol, where they lay bricks. How valiant they are to me, laying the foundation for our nation's greatest building. A great testament and symbol of union is what it is, and they construct it proudly."

"And now you're going to war to preserve the Union," Ellie whispered. "Oh, Mr. Mehan—"

"Mike, call me Mike—"

"I think you're wonderful, Mike."

Mike chucked another rock, and allowed himself a modest smile. "A man must fight for something, or he must fight against himself."

"And does your father have a command, now?"

"Does he?" Mike laughed. "Try to keep him at home! He's ferocious in battle."

He put an arm about her shoulders, and pointed her ahead with a wave of his hand. "Picture him, Ellie," (and so she did) "a tall, broad-shouldered man with the mane of a lion, white as moonlight, a warrior-poet striking at his enemy, laying waste all around. Fearless, he feels no pain, the cries of his foes touch him not, he is the whirlwind."

He stopped speaking and let the air cool his cheeks. Up the river came a barge, its deck covered with the shadowy forms of silent soldiers from the Union Army's camp at Falmouth. Ellie pressed one hand over her heart.

"I feel a great honor in listening to you speak," she said in a low voice. "It makes me feel proud to be American, to hear how you talk. Your father must be so proud to know what you'll do to protect this country."

Mike grinned. "You should see the effect it has on him. Nothing matters to him more than the land of his birth. Why, when I left home today, he could barely speak, so moved was he."

And Mike started to laugh, while the barge of silent soldiers went silently by.

THE IRISH BRIGADE

1

A THOUSAND AND half a thousand more years ago, the Fianna were the soldiers of Ireland, with Finn mac Cumhail at their head. And the ages wore on, and the rough stones of Ireland were worn smooth by the tears of the Fianna's families. Badb, the great gory goddess of war, washed soldiers' clothes in the moss-rocked streams by the fields of battle, and each man who saw her wash his garments knew his blood was forfeit, and threw himself ever more fiercely into the fight.

And never was there any halt of soldiering or crying, even when Ireland had disappeared in the mist beyond the American horizon. So when the North called upon its newcomers to fight, Colonel

Meagher, the new Finn mac Cumhail, raised his regiments in New York, and the Irish regiments from Massachusetts, Pennsylvania, New Jersey, and the United States regiments of Washington, and all joined together to form the Irish Brigade.

Then were the Fianna marching again to the Lands of Badb, and my cursed brother with them.

And nothing will suit the Fianna so much but that they be first and fiercest in the fight, and show the greatest valor and the least amount of pain.

So they rush from the revel to join the parade
For the van is the right of the Irish Brigade.

2

MARCH CAME IN my dreams like the soft wind that swiftly turns bitter, and I stared many a night at my candle in the small room I had at the top of the Shinny. Or I'd sit working over my lace, building and building the delicate net rope, and as my fingers worked their well-known stitches I'd close my eyes and see Mike, how he stepped so light along the camp's corduroy streets, how he ducked into a tent to join a game of cards and drink a round of oh-be-joyful moonshine, how he drilled with his fellows in the muddy meadow where the trees were felled all around for miles and miles, a forest of stumps the witnesses to Mike's training in war.

I'd see him shoulder a gun, and drop to his knee, and sight along the bayonet at the advancing lines. And I'd try to see the Confederate lines, how they would advance, but that was where my dreams could not go.

General Hooker, the third general to have command and charge of the Army of the Potomac, sat mumbling his pipestem and dreaming of Richmond, the rebel capital in Virginia. This, while General Lee jigged about Virginia and dreamed of his home in Arlington, across the Potomac from Washington, the Federal capital. How laughable to have two such generals, each wishing to be where the other was. Each commanded squadrons, regiments, brigades, corps, entire armies of Irish boys, for the Irish fought for the Confederacy, too, and faced the Irish of the North on fields like Fredericksburg.

At that battle, boys of the Union Irish Brigade, commanded by the second general, General Burnside, were mowed down by the Irish boys of the 24th Georgia, melting like snow upon the ground before the advance. How glorious, cried the generals, weeping with pride. See how the Irish fight! See how well they die! The fame of the Irish

Brigade grew with each man lost, and was as wide as the sea and tall as the masts in Galway Bay by the end of the battle. What matter that the battle was such a catastrophe for the Federal troops that Burnside resigned his command and Lincoln put in Hooker? Glory was the Irish boys'.

It was at the Battle of Fredericksburg that Whitman's brother was wounded, and so brought Mr. Walt to Washington to meet me. Thus do all our dreams mingle and breathe together. Generals Hooker and Lee, Walt Whitman, the Fianna, Mike, and me, all dreaming and fighting together.

Hooker's devoutest dream, beyond Richmond, was more men, more men: Give me more men. Mr. Lincoln, give me more men so I may take Richmond and lay waste the rebel capital. And though Lincoln was dreaming of a general who would let Richmond starve to death and instead go after that dancing Lee, he gave Hooker more men.

" 'The Congress has passed the Conscription Act,' " read Finn from the newspaper at the Shinny on March 4. "They've done it now, and can draft anyone they like. Aliens exempt."

The fellows at the bar gave themselves winks of congratulation.

"I'll go if I like," Colm Peel declared in the thickest Dublin accent this side of the Atlantic.

"But the draft board can go hang if they try to force me into the war."

"They'll draft aliens soon enough." Dooley looked sour. "S'long as this war goes on they'll be needing men."

"Yes, to replace the ones they've broken and can't play with anymore," muttered I to myself.

Milky Wesley was cradling Snatcher in his big hands. The terrier fixed me with a beady glance. "What d'you hear from your brother, Mairhe? Have they got him broken in yet?"

"Not a word, Milky, as you well know."

Milky included the other fellows in his knowing look. "No doubt he's liking it. That Mike is a natural soldier."

"Don't say so!" I whisked a half-empty glass out from under his nose, and left Wesley gaping dry as a fish and the dog flat-eared with surprise.

"Teach you to get on the wrong side of Mairhe Mehan," Dooley laughed. "Will you buy another, Milky?"

I stood by the window to steady my breathing, and watched the twilight coming down. My fingers were idle and itched for the lace that was my constant occupation. Such yards I had, yet such spiderweb stuff it was. But it was making and it was holding together and it was twining and binding and I could see it. I could hold it and know I had fashioned it tight and strong and beautiful. The thread alone was so weak, so easy to snap. But when it was netted together with itself, oh, so strong it was!

But even as I turned to fetch my handwork there came a commotion and a clamor from outdoors, and I bent my gaze to see down the street. A riderless horse, harness flying, came trampling down our dead-end alley toward the Shinny, and a whole screaming crowd after it. The men in the bar yanked open the door and crowded together to see what the yelling was about.

The black horse was screaming and rearing, trying to find a way out of the box it was in, and the crowd of men and soldiers pressed forward, close to the flying hooves, and Snatcher darting back and forth all the while barking mad as a demon. All was dim and shadowy in the alley, but the sky above was still bright and clear, if the horse could only fly up to it.

"Get it, goddammit!" a fat and sweating sergeant yelled. "Control that beast, wrangler!"

A small man tried to duck in to grab the reins, but the horse was white-eyed and sidling and tossing about too wild to capture. The army wranglers were bringing horses from the West every day to break for cavalry mounts, and the barns all over

Washington were filled with half-wild horses. I'd seen the wranglers breaking these horses in the big corrals, and seen a man trampled, but this was a first, an unbroken horse tearing up the alley outside the Shinny.

While the shouting and barking continued to lash the horse wilder, and the men from the Shinny laid bets on who'd get the best of the fight, the wrangler darted in again to grab the reins and took a hoof in the middle of his back. He went down under the hooves, and the sergeant whipped his hat off in fury.

"Control that animal or shoot it!" he screamed, pushing two soldiers forward. "Get that wrangler out and subdue the animal!"

The horse was dancing and shying and unwilling to step on the unconscious wrangler. As it backed into a corner the men in the doorway of the Shinny stepped out into the alley for a better look, leaving the door wide open.

And all in a flash the maddened horse lowered his head and bolted into the Shinny itself, crashing into tables and skidding in the sawdust of the wooden floor. Crockery and glass smashed all around it, and the men poured back inside in astonishment to see an unbroken horse break their saloon to bits.

"Get that thing out!" Dooley yelled, and Mrs.

Dooley took one peek through the kitchen door and disappeared with a shriek.

The sergeant stepped in and shot the horse in the shoulder with his pistol. The animal screamed again and went down thrashing. Then the sergeant stepped closer and shot the creature between the eyes.

Then all was silence, but for Snatcher barking, barking at the dead animal's bleeding head in the smoky, rising dust.

3

WHAT WITH THE destruction and devastation of the furnishings of the place, and the blood and the dead horse in the middle of the wreckage, and all so appalled they had a dry and churchlike feeling of doom and left for home, Dooley was irate. Furthermore he forbade us to make any inroads in picking up the place, for he was determined to have compensation for his loss from the Army and make them dispose of the carcase, though Mr. O'Callahan was all for butchering it and Milky Wesley wanted it for dog's meat.

And so all cleared out before the barman's shouts of outrage, and the Dooleys and I sat in the kitchen in a dire silence, for the weight of the dead horse oppressed us all. Mrs. Dooley and I made a dinner of sorts, and Dooley muttered his anger into his plate and ticked off Quartermaster, Attorney-General, War Department on his thick fingers.

In the morning I found it had not been a dream, though I stepped into the saloon with a hope that it would be all as usual.

"Disgusting, I say," Mrs. Dooley said from the far door. She stood wringing her hands, sick to leave such a sight uncleaned. In the middle of the room lay the horse, and the bloody sawdust around it hard and dark.

"Get on, Mairhe," she added. "Dooley'll be all over the city today trying to get satisfaction of the government, which I doubt not he'll never see. Go see your Da, take him our love."

When I didn't move, she shooed me angrily away, and I stepped unwilling into the street.

A clear morning, and the smell of mud from the Tiber was ripe and mossy. I had not been to St. Aloysius to see my Da since he'd gone in on the church's charity, and I had no wish to do so now, so I turned myself toward the center of the city, looking for some sight that would cheer me more than a horse lying dead in a saloon. I knew I'd not find it watching a man fight against his own memories and dreams.

Well, there were those things about the day that could have brought me cheer. Early March it was, but there was a tenderness in the air. Folks were out walking, and though the city streets were rutted worse than ever with the artillery wagons and ambulances and all, the mud was soft and yielding, and not so cruel to the feet. One man called to another, and a mother called her son, and two small girls laughed on a doorstep as they scraped mud from their shoes. The stamp and jingle of horses drawing gigs down the avenues, and the squeal of a pig chased by boys, and cows lowing as a drover herded them along, and the ringing of a hammer from a smithy—these sounds all beckoned me forward in a daydream of the county fair of Sligo, where Matthew Mehan would fight all comers in the ring.

And oh, couldn't I see it so plain, hear the bleating of sheep and smell the bay and see my father all in his prime, all in his prime. This loss of things, this angry breaking apart of what I loved and what was best around me, had plagued me all through the years. And at that moment it was so awful to me that I must stop and look at my own two hands. I must clutch my hands together and feel my fingers, to see that I myself was not falling into shards and fragments, or tearing down the things around me as I fell, as a tall tree falls in the forest and destroys the things around it.

But no, I was not broken, though I felt as slender and drawn as a thread.

A gig rattled by beside me in the street, startling me out of my dream. Still gripping and holding my own hands, I walked on. I walked on until I stood within sight of the Capitol, where all was building, building, building.

Can a person be two things at once? Can we believe in one thing strongly and equally in its opposite? Can we believe in union, and in independence as well? Can we be both American and not American, Irish and not Irish? Must we choose?

Whitman, now, that man could embrace in his big arms equally the Michigander and the Georgian, the man of Tennessee and the man of Massachusetts, the farmer of Carolina and the factory worker of New York, the woodman, the shopgirl, father and brother—all things equally within him and he carried them all so light. Easy for him to say!

But I found myself all alone looking at the Capitol, not knowing what I was nor wanted to be.

4

SAINT PATRICK'S DAY, and wasn't there a wild Irish bang-up everywhere? The Shinny was restored, though Dooley himself had fallen into a black humor from which nothing could persuade him. Yet the saloon was thick with Irish folk, and music filled the air, and I feared I'd wear out my shoes from treading from bar to tables with dripping mugs of ale.

And there was a laughing, dancing, hand-clapping roar of the rollicking crowd at the Shinny, while in Kelly's Ford, Virginia, the Saint Patrick's festivities were of a different nature. There, three thousand Federal horse troops under W. W. Averell were riding to cross the Rappahannock for to engage the Confederates at Culpeper. The column of cavalry raised a fine dust in the spring air, and the dust settled on the blue shoulders and tilted blue hats of the riders. Blue jays carked and screeched between the trees at the jingle of the bits and the clank of sabers against stirrups and the clink of horseshoe on stone.

I say it was like the clank and clink of mug against mug as I set them down at the crowded tables, and the finest particles of sawdust from the floor drifting in among the smoke, and one man called to another to take out his fiddle, 'twas time for a tune.

In the column a captain raised his hand, and the jogging and jostling of horses came to a huddling halt behind him. A horse snorted and tossed its head. One man bethought himself of a pipe, and another man wondered on the beautiful white arms and throat of his young wife back with her family in Illinois, and yet another scratched his chigger bites and looked across the ford into the farther woods. The sun slanted down on Kelly's Ford, where the Rappahannock sparkled and gleamed over the shallows, and the mud along its bank held the dainty dancing prints of raccoon and possum. The horses shifted from foot to foot, smelling the water, and turned their ears one way and another against the flies.

And so the men in the Shinny shifted their chairs about, and a table or two was shoved aside to make room for the dancing. Colm Peel took up a bow, and Finn took a whistle from his pocket, while Milky Wesley began to drum on a tabletop with a galloping beat.

The beat, so soft at first, was clearer to hear through the woods whence Averell's cavalry came. The horses beneath them were the first to be sure, for their ears pricked and their necks arched, even as Averell gave the command to wheel about and re-form with the ford at their backs. Up the woodland road came the rebels, fierce as rebels, swearing to keep the Federals from crossing Kelly's Ford. Jeb Stuart's dreaded Virginia Cavalry was riding to pound the Federals.

And so it began, with Colm Peel taking the beat from Milky Wesley, and Finn joining a skirling little reel that ran above the fiddler's bow. Around them, the men clapped their hands and tapped their feet, and when the tune settled into one they all knew, didn't they sing? And didn't they dance and carry on, and the smoke and the kicked-up sawdust thicker and the clapping and stomping louder and louder by the minute, and even the fiddler whirling with the rest and the shouts and all mingling withal?

Limbs flying, mouths agape, bodies jerking this way and that—such noise and confusion was as natural to battle as the blood and the litter of cartridge boxes and dropped hats and dented canteens and dead men. The Union troops formed themselves around a small farm as the Confederates pressed them hard. Horses trampled new-furrowed fields, the flags were carried first here and then there, officers shouting from horseback and vaulting fences, the artillery bombardments raising fountains of dirt and stone, the wounded, crying men carried behind chicken coop and hog pen and springhouse. Shot horses kicked and struggled in bloody mud, and cries for water, please, water, as the sun heated the ground, rose like a groaning choir. A man, sitting foolishly in a mudhole, held his blasted hand in his other hand and looked up.

"Help me, Mairhe. Give me a hand."

Mrs. Dooley took me by the arm, and led me to the kitchen. "It's all I can do to lift this kettle of praties off the stove," said she.

I had a great urge to help her and return to the bar, and throw myself into the celebration with the others. For it is true that none can listen to Irish tunes without knowing she's Irish, and wanting to pound that truth into the floor with her feet. So I hurried after Mrs. Dooley, and we two dashed the praties from their boiling kettle, and then I was out again with the folks who had no part of America or its war in them.

"Give us a song I can do, Mr. Peel," I begged as I stepped near that man.

And he brought a cease-fire in a moment by raising both bow and fiddle in the air. "Boys, be still. Mairhe Mehan will favor us with a song."

" 'Nancy Whiskey'!"

" 'The Girls of Galway'!"

"Nay, make it *'A Ghaoth Andeas!'* " I said.

The laughter stopped and Peel tapped the strings with his bow. " 'O South Wind!' "

With the men around me, and Peel and Finn to accompany me, I sang the Irish words, *A Connachta an tsóidh, an tsuilt is an spóirt, I nimirt is in n-ól an fhíona, Sin chugaibh mo phóg ar rith ins a' ród. Leigim le seól gaoith eí. . . .* Oh joyful Connacht, home of sport and wine, I send my kiss rushing down the road to you, I send it on the wings of the wind. I live in splendor, yet am I drawn home to you when I hear the music of the pipes.

The Gaelic was rough and salty in my mouth and the Shinny men sang tunefully with me as I closed my eyes tight and tried to dream of Ireland, tried to make it the dream of my heart and let the south wind blow me there.

But I couldn't, you see, for all I had of Ireland was dreams of it, and they weren't even my dreams to begin with. And when you have nothing at all, a dream will only lull you into dreaming forever.

That I would not do.

LINCOLN'S HORNPIPE

1

HORNPIPE: A SOLO sailor's dance. Imagine a man kicking his heels first to one side and then the other as he squeezes and draws on the wheezing concertina, and there you have the very picture.

On a fine Saturday morning early in April, Mr. Lincoln made his gloomy, black, and stork-legged way to the Washington Navy Yard, there to board his little steamboat, the *Carrie Martin*. He stood at the prow as the boat chugged its way down the Potomac—a beak-nosed scarecrow of a figurehead, the light dappling up onto his dark face from the water—and folded his arms.

In this stance did he make his riverine way to see General Hooker at Fredericksburg, to see if he might persuade his commander to ask General Lee for a dance.

General McClellan had not engaged Lee and so General Burnside cut in. Yet General Burnside had not engaged Lee, and so General Hooker cut in. Now General Hooker, damnably, would not engage Lee!

"Forget Richmond," muttered the President under his breath as the banks of army-trampled Virginia farmland slipped past the *Carrie Martin*. "The enemy is not *at* Richmond, sir, but there, ahead of us."

The *pocka-pocka-pocka* of the little boat's steam engine caused the gray, beaky wading birds to fly up in a gawky confusion, flapping wide, ungainly wings from the muddy greenery at the river's edges, their long legs dangling behind them. Lincoln watched them, brooding, and again muttered in sardonic tones, "Forget Richmond, sir. Or if you will not use the Army, let me borrow it at least."

And one week later, back went the President, standing at the prow of the *Carrie Martin*, gloomier than ever, still dancing solo. *Pocka-pocka-pocka.* General Hooker would not engage General Lee. The South only survived because of Lee, and Hooker would not take him on.

In camp, Mike was cleaning his fingernails with

a knife, and basking in the attention of questions that bombarded him. For the President had reviewed the troops while he was struggling to persuade Hooker, and Mike had let it be known that he was a Washington boy and had seen Lincoln many times, even stopped in at the President's House at a public reception or two. Mike's company was quartered near one from Wisconsin, and the Irish boyos were peeling money from the farm kids in poker.

"Sure, haven't I seen him riding to and fro the Soldiers' Home, where he spends the summer months?" Mike said, leaning back against a crate of ammunition. "Sits a horse about as well as a sack of praties does."

"D'you suppose he noticed us in the review?" asked Willie Arendt, the cards slack in his hands, and his mouth slack, too.

Mike caught a glimpse of Willie's deuces and treys and gave the boy a saintly smile. "Who could help noticing what a fine figure you are, Willie? Sure and the President was that impressed. Your worth is plain for all to see."

With that Mike put down his hand—full house, queen high—and picked up Willie's stake. Mike tossed the coins into the air and caught them as they fell.

Willie was dismayed, but never doubted Mike played straight. "Again? You've got some luck with cards, Mehan."

"I do, I do."

Donny Gallagher, Mike's mate, dragged his cap down over his mouth to stifle a laugh and stretched his feet in his too-tight boots. "He's a rare one, that's certain."

"Tell about Washington," begged another Wisconsin lad, named Johnny, whose hair was so blond it shone white in the dim of the tent.

Mike pretended to consider, and took a pull from his canteen. "It's a city that grabs a man—"

"Is that right?" Johnny asked.

"When he steps into the mud that's ankle-deep," Mike added, wiping his mouth on the back of his hand. "And never did you see such a collection of proud officers—leaning against the bar at Willard's Hotel."

"And girls. The Washington girls are pretty, isn't that so?" asked young Willie.

Mike's nimble fingers now made quick work with the cards. "The girls are sweet, I cannot tell a lie. And my sister the sweetest of all, for she wept a rain of tears when I left for the war."

"Proud of you, eh?"

"Not to say proud, no . . ." Mike drawled.

Willie nodded. "Fearful of your life, is that it?"

"To tell you the truth," and here Mike lowered his voice, and leaned forward so his hat tipped over one eye, "I believe she'd come track me down if she knew how to get a pass to cross the picket lines, and would march in here and take me home bodily to the bosom of my family. For we neither of us can write more than our names, you know, so she'd never try to persuade with a letter. But she wants me home, boys, I guarantee that."

Johnny slapped his knees. "Picture it, a girl coming down here to an army camp and trying to talk you into anything, Mike!"

"But his sister," Willie protested. "A fellow has to listen to his sister."

At that, Mike swept up the cards. "That's enough play, boys, I've got to see a man about a horse."

He stooped to leave the tent. Above his head, the clear sky blazed, and at his feet, the corduroy street of saplings laid side by side by side stretched at right angles through a city of dingy tents. Wherever he looked were regimental flags, state flags, the colors of all the troops of the great and stagnating Army of the Potomac. The stench of the latrines held away from him, and he breathed deep the smell of mud and bad coffee and damp clothes, and heard the sound of coughing rattle from one end of camp to another.

And did he wish his sister came? Did he give her

a thought as he went down the street to the barbering tent for to get himself a shave? Or did he think only of army matters, that he'd go mad sitting in camp all spring, endlessly parading and drilling and marching in columns, walking picket lines, waiting for Hooker to make up his mind?

For if he could not fight, why was he here? If he could not prove himself an American by fighting, why should he stay?

2

SO AFTER ALL the grieving and despair I'd known, watching in silence while all around me fell to pieces and I not lifting a finger to stop them, then at last did I decide what course to take. A pass I must secure, an official pass from a military authority, an office of the government. The government was all around me, but I'd no more notion where to go than a cat does.

Thus it was that in my spare moments I took to haunting the hospitals in the last days of April, dancing from foot to foot, my hands clasped before me, or alternately caught behind my back. For I had my own hornpipe to dance, and wait through. And as the days increased in the spring, and the fruit sellers plied the avenues, and the salesmen hawked their patent medicines and five-cent books, I paced beneath the leafing trees outside one hospital and another, waiting for a glimpse of Mr. Walt.

And then, outside the Patent Office hospital one day, there he was, striding down the steps in a queer wide sombrero and a pair of cordovan boots, his shirt open at the throat like a stevedore's and his pockets stuffed and bulging.

I doubted he would remember me, but I knew of no one else close to the Army. I stepped out to meet him.

"Mairhe Mehan, is it?" said he.

"Yes, sir."

He beamed at me, his eyes bright behind his bushy beard. He smelled of coffee and bacon. "Come to work in the hospital, have you?"

I stepped backward so suddenly I nearly fell. "Sir, not at all, but to ask you for help."

"Well, then, walk with me down to Pennsylvania Avenue, as I have some commissions to carry out at the Capitol."

He set off, arms swinging, and I must hurry to catch him up.

"Mr. Walt, I need a pass to get me out of the city and conduct me across the picket lines at the army camp."

Just as suddenly as he started, he stopped, and

looked at me keenly. "I don't take you for a camp follower, nor do you need a pass for that. So what's your business, Mairhe Mehan, and why do you think I can help you in it?"

An organ grinder began to play across the street, and the smell of roasting chestnuts came to me on the air as I waited for the heat to leave my face.

"This is the way of it. My brother's gone for a soldier, believing my father and me to provide for one another's comfort. But my father's mind broke down just as my brother left, and he has been taken in on charity, and I've no support but my brother. So I would go and tell him that, and have him return to Washington and save him from this war."

Mr. Walt took up his walking again. "And are you living on the streets, Mairhe, or on charity yourself?"

And then was I crying and could not help it. "Sir, I know I am poor and have no claim on you, but neither do I deserve that you always reproach me. It is true I live at the Shinny now, where I am the barmaid and so work for my place. But I feel every day the pain and the woe that this war is bringing. I feel it in my dreams at night and during the day. I can't hold so much misfortune in me without my brother to help me, and I know no one else I can ask for aid."

Mr. Walt dragged a handkerchief from his

pocket, and handed it to me as we walked on. I wiped my face. It smelled of sweat and chloroform, and I knew he'd wiped soldiers' eyes and brows and cheeks with it and so it lapped my tears, too. A barouche rattled by on taut springs, a well-dressed lady inside. Mr. Walt stood to watch it go, and then did he give me a smile.

"I feel it too, Mairhe," said he at last. "I feel it every day and night, just as you do. That's why I go to the hospitals, and try to help those poor boys who suffer so much. I feel it does me some good to do them some good."

"Don't ask me to go into the hospitals," I begged. "I can't bear it."

"I believe you could."

I shook my head, and couldn't answer. We came abreast of the organ grinder, who dolefully turned the crank of his organ and kept his eyes on the ground. Mr. Walt and I went on by him, and the mechanical tune faded behind us.

"I won't press you. Where's your father, now?"

"St. Aloysius, our church that now is an army hospital."

He nodded, and took off his sombrero to wipe his brow with his sleeve. "How is he?"

When I did not answer, Mr. Walt jammed his hat back on his head and took my arm. "Come on, girl."

And so he pulled me through the pretty April

streets of Washington until they turned to the muddy April streets of Swampoodle and the clock tower of St. Aloysius rose before us. Ambulances and mortuary wagons came and went as always, for as the spring brought floods and mud and warmer weather, so it also brought skirmishes and casualties. Mr. Walt paused to let two stretcher-bearers carry their bloody load into the main door of the church, and then went in.

This left me displaced entirely. Here was I, in my own Swampoodle, on the outside of things and apart. Down the street came the sounds of hammering and sawing from a coffin-maker's shop. I stood in a shadow, and watched the ambulance men discharge their duty. Faint groans and cries came from the wagons; the sunlight was dazzling outdoors, but the open door of the church led into darkness, like a crypt. I watched each moaning, wounded soldier as he was carried from the bright day into the dark, and then, stepping out of the black entrance was Mr. Walt, and my Da.

Old he looked, old and broken as he'd never looked before. He followed meekly at Mr. Walt's side, blinking in the sun like a pale shadow of Mr. Walt, wondering and tipping his face up at the bright sky. My heart coiled within my breast.

"Oh, Da," I said, going forward.

"Is it Deirdre, then?"

"No, Da. Her daughter and yours. Mairhe." I put his hand to my face.

"Mairhe. Mairhe." Da turned his head as the stretcher-bearers passed by us. He frowned. "They bring these boys here every day, I don't understand it atall. This is a church. Have they no sense of holiness?"

"Da—"

"Mairhe, where's Mike? Where's your brother?"

"He's in the Army, Da, but I'm going to get him out. We need him, you and I, and I'm going to bring him back so we'll be a family again, and we'll go west, and we'll start new."

"Connacht is as west as you may get," Da said with a laugh. "You may get west of Sligo, but not by much. Are you saying we'll go to Connemara? The Mehans in Connemara, now there's something to think on."

I felt Mr. Walt's gaze on us so full of tender pity that I couldn't meet his eyes. Through the door of the church behind us came Father Wiget, squinting in the sunlight.

"Matthew, how do you like to see your daughter?" the chaplain asked.

"Father, I want you to have a word with my son, Michael. He's about here somewhere, mark me. He never minds what I say, but he'll listen to you."

"Come along in, Matthew. He may be somewhere

inside." Father Wiget, with one arm about my father's shoulders, led the way back into the darkness of the church.

Mr. Walt and I stood where we were, the hammering from the coffin-makers echoing in the street. The pounding of the hammers resounded from the walls and roof of the church, pouring down like a rain of hammering, as though St. Aloysius itself were being fashioned into a coffin and the lid being nailed down.

"You oughtn't have brought me."

"Maybe not. I make any number of blunders when I try to do good." Mr. Walt sighed.

I turned away, for to find my path to the Shinny. Mr. Walt called after me.

"I'll see what I can learn for you. Don't hope for too much."

I looked back briefly. "I never do."

3

IF I TELL you there was a box at the opera, with people seated within it, I may tell you where around the box those people sat and what they watched, and those are the facts of the case. But where's the truth of it? A man seated on a red chair across an uncrossable stretch of carpet from the red-haired woman he loves may be holding her hand in his heart. And although the woman in velvet who lifts the gilded opera glasses to her eyes and parts her lips sits beside her mother and even whispers kindly to her from time to time, she may be miles from her in spirit. And though the opera upon the stage may be found in the libretto, the opera each watches is a private affair.

Or I may tell you that the aeronauts ascended the sky in their delicate hot air balloons, and gazed far afield at the enemy army camps, and telegraphed their reports down the long, long wire to the ground. Ten units of cavalry here. One battalion deployed thus. The ground is level and open, rising to the west. But does the aeronaut's message contain the dismay he feels as he beholds the blasted woodlands to the south? And does he know that the man on the ground who decodes his telegram has three brothers in that army? And do they either one hear the voices of the men in that camp who clean their guns and write letters home, and slowly turn the pages of their Bibles?

So is history to be found in the heart and memory and the imagination, not in the photographer's glass plate or the journalist's wired message to the editor.

So these dreams are true, I tell you, as true as anything else.

And if I tell you I kept my brother alive by dreaming of him, that is true too.

How else could I fill the days of April, waiting to hear from Mr. Walt, waiting to know if I could go to my brother, if I could send to his commander and pull him from the ranks? I danced a perpetual hornpipe back and forth and back and forth in one place, waiting, waiting for the music to stop, making my lace without end, and wishing not to think of my Da.

So as the month drew to its close, and Lincoln proclaimed a national day of prayer for the restoration of the Union, I dreamed of the murmur of advance moving through camp like a wind moving through leaves, louder as it neared and growing more distinct. I dreamed Mike looking up from his cards, and giving grave Gallagher a glance.

"This is it, boys," Gallagher announced.

"How'd you know it?" Mike asked. He jerked a thumb out the tent. "Nothing but noise and shouting, so far."

A corporal leaned his head in under the canvas. "They're blowing assembly in a minute, lads. Strike camp. Looks like Lincoln finally lit a fire under Hooker's boots."

"Mother of God, it's about time, too," Mike swore, and rolled from his perch and landed on the ground. He grabbed up his hat and slapped it across one palm. "Let's go a-soldiering."

And out stepped Mike from under the shade of the mildewed canvas tent, into the April sunshine and mud of the camp. The quartermaster wagons were already rolling, the drovers whistling and whipping, and a mule bucking as it backed into its harness, and a brace of men putting their shoulders to the wheels of an artillery cannon to dislodge it from the mud, and a man emptying a coffeepot into a cook fire, and above the smell of army camp was a soft breeze blowing toward the Rappahannock and battle, boys, battle!

So rank and file assembled themselves into their units, and the flashy officers paraded on their arching horses, and the shouts of command passed from division commander to brigadier general to colonel to captain, and the soldiers all hearing the echoes not dwindling but growing louder and louder all about—forward!

"And if your sister could see you now?" Gallagher asked of Mike.

Mike patted the canteen at his hip, tested the straps of his rucksack, weighed his rifle. "If my dear sister could see me now, she'd be carping and complaining on something, I promise you that. For she's always in a black mood and wouldn't see the joy of this moment."

With a squint around at the marching mass, Gallagher spit into the mud, which was a good mud, soft underfoot but not so deep the wagons would roll it to ankle-turning ruts. "Does she not appreciate what we're fighting for?"

"What we're fighting for," Mike repeated, eyes ahead on the marching blue backs. "What we're fighting for . . . No, by God, she does not."

4

MR. WALT CAME into the Shinny, breathless and with biscuit crumbs in his beard. "Mairhe, I have been much about on this business of yours and I may have some hope for you."

I poured him a glass of beer and set it before him careful and slow. "Tell me."

"I've done a good amount of clerking at the Paymaster General's office—it's how I earn my room and board—and I put your case to a friend of mine there. He arranged for you to go with me to the War Department to plead your case and see if we can't get your brother discharged."

I stared at his face, watching him speak these words.

"Now, Mairhe. Come now."

And without further fuss or falter, we went out the door making for the War Department at Pennsylvania Avenue and Seventeenth Street. I didn't say a word as we hurried along, didn't answer as Mr. Walt pointed out the tender lilacs blooming in a dooryard or called to my ear the queer high calls of the drovers as they yipped and hied a herd of cattle onto the lawn of the President's House. My thoughts were of Mike only, and of getting him out.

So Mr. Walt understood me and ceased calling my attention to this spring herald or that, and only led the way to the office where we were to go. Artillery cannon flanked the building, and soldiers guarded the door. We went into a moving mass of blue uniforms and the high echoing confusion of men's voices filling the high hall and the tramping of feet. Mr. Walt tucked my hand firm under his arm, and in his easy way asked to make way, and conveyed us through the voiceful clamorous crowd to an officer seated at a desk, beset on all sides by soldiers and officers and aides.

"Not now, goddammit," the officer said, brushing aside a sheaf of papers thrust before him and resuming his parley with a beefy man in a stained uniform. "—Chancellorsville, that area, find the appropriate maps to take to the Secretary's office—"

We stood before him, waiting to be noticed. Mr. Walt was still and silent, his white-haired, white-bearded, white-shirted figure standing out against the dark blue sea like a lighthouse.

"Yes, what is it?" the officer asked abruptly. "This isn't the right place for casualty lists, you know."

"Where do we find Major Hanford?" Mr. Walt asked.

The officer pointed, relieved to be rid of us so easily. "Third floor, that way. No, not now," he snapped again at an aide at his side.

We went up the right-hand stairs that echoed with bootheels and military mutterings and the jingle of cavalry spurs. The place was a murmurous mass, active as a kicked-over anthill. The uniformed officers and soldiers gave us only hurried passing glances as we went up: the white-haired bearish man, and me, a black-haired Irish girl with dark eyes large and staring.

At the landing, two officers with gold braid stood in silhouette at the window, the bars outside the glass cutting them into pieces like stained glass. They looked up as we came, and one drew the white gloves from his belt and ran them through his hand, and then inclined his head to his fellow officer and looked at us not again. We turned onto the next flight up. My heart was pounding. The staircase switched back and forth as it climbed, and men continually bore down on us as we battled upstream against the current.

"Don't be frightened, Mairhe," Mr. Walt said, wondering around at the noise and frantic action. "Your petition will be heard."

When at last we reached the proper floor, he led me by the hand down the corridor. Oaken doors loomed beside us, and opened here and there or shut abruptly. Aides with papers and dispatch cases went in and out.

"Is it always so—so all of a frenzy?" I whispered.

Mr. Walt looked cautiously around, and bent his head down to mine. "Something may be happening soon. I don't know— Ah, here we are."

He pulled me along, and I followed through the door into an office. The appointments were richer than any I'd ever seen, the polished desks, the silk flag, the Turkey carpet on the floor. Mr. Walt beckoned to me where I stood like a statue.

"Now, Miss Mehan," spoke the man at a desk, this Major Hanford. He didn't look up at me, but at the paper before him. His fingers were ink-stained, his desk littered with dispatches and lists and ledgers. "What is the nature of your petition? I have your brother's name and his regiment before me. What is it you wish to ask?"

"He's gone away into the Army thinking my Da and I'd look out for each other—"

"And?"

"And my Da took ill and is taken into the parish on charity, sir, and I am on my own. I've no other family."

Major Hanford looked up. Light from the window put a sheen on his sandy hair and mustache, but did nothing to light his eyes. "Was your brother a conscript?"

I clutched my hands. "No, sir, he's Irish. Exempt from the draft, sir. He enlisted in January."

"Hmm. If he'd been drafted that would be one thing. But if he chose to enlist—"

"But sir, he didn't know how he'd be leaving me," I whispered. "Didn't know what his leaving would do to our Da. He wouldn't have signed on if he knew."

The sound of tramping feet grew loud in the hallway, passed the door, and grew faint. I saw Mike walking away from my Da, and my Da putting his fist through a window, and all the time Mike knowing what he'd done to us. And then I knew he'd broken my heart as carelessly as he'd broken anything else.

Around me, the edges of my vision began to fade.

"What's wrong with the girl?"

"She looks faint."

"Can't you do something?"

"I'm well enough," I said. I gripped the edges of the polished desk, and my fingers left smears. I noticed the officer noticing them.

"Yes, well, let me look into this matter," he said, tapping some papers together. He didn't look at me. "Come back in . . . shall we say ten days."

"Ten days?"

"There are many cases to be reviewed, Miss Mehan. Yours will receive its attention in its time. And it happens this is a particularly bad time to be asking."

"The Army's advancing?" Mr. Walt asked, keening forward.

"Good day to you."

"Sir? Will you get him out?"

Mr. Walt took my arm and led me out of the room. "We can only ask so much at one time."

Out in the hall I stopped and looked up at him. I could feel tears in my eyes. "Why'd he do it to me?"

"The Army has these regulations—" Mr. Walt began.

"Oh, wirra, wirra! No." I shook my head and went blindly for the stairs. "No."

He fell into step beside me. I ducked my face away, but he was a man who knew weeping when he saw it, silent or no. He walked ahead of me, and the blue resonating crowds parted around us and closed behind us as water closes around a moving bubble, until we came out into the sunshine of the avenue.

"What is it, Mairhe? What's happened?"

I put one hand to shield my eyes, and dropped my head for I couldn't bear it that my brother had done this to me, left me with nothing at all to dream of.

"My brother knew what he was doing," I said in a dull voice. A soldier brushed my shoulder in passing, knocking me aside. "He knew what he was doing and didn't care."

"Perhaps he didn't know. If he loves you, he wouldn't have done it."

I looked up at Mr. Walt. "Ah, but that's it, isn't it? And if he doesn't love me, what have I got? Not a thing in this world."

"You've got your country," he solemnly said.

"Jesus and Mary, you don't understand it at all, do you! I haven't got any damned country, have I? I don't belong to anyone or anything or anyplace. If I am divided from my brother, I am in pieces. I am a fragment. I have no more substance than a dream that's gone."

Mr. Walt stood there like a rock, like a tree, like a house, just looking and looking at me until I was so angry I hit him in the arm. And again he only looked at me, so I walked away from him, back to Swampoodle, the Irish bog that I called home, there to close my eyes to what I'd seen and keep my dreaming deep.

For what could I have known of that furor and frantic flow of men and officers within the War Department? What could I have known but what I dreamed of my brother, as his regiment moved up the Virginia road to Chancellorsville, which was nothing more than a single grand house, and removed the rebuking Chancellor women who defied them from the colonnaded porch?

And General Hooker made the place his headquarters, there to wait for Lee in the open ground, at the advantage. A hundred and thirty thousand men of the Army of the Potomac, invincible, unmovable, thick on the ground in their legions, waiting for Lee's small barefoot and butternut army to fall before them. They could not lose. The time was come to crush the foe, to salt his wells, and put his face in the dust.

And when the battle began it wasn't one battle but many over the first budding days of May, in the primrose woods and on the buttercup hilltops, with cavalry and entrenchments and gun-smoking moonlight and Hooker incredibly giving up the advantage at every turn, and Lee continually dividing and dividing again his small forces to shatter Hooker.

Mike sat with his comrades at a fire as the sun rose on the second day of battle, cooking coffee on the misty ground and marveling that they were alive, and a fox sprang out of the thicket and ran straight through their fire, scattering sparks as red as its tail and upsetting the coffeepot into the flames with a hiss.

And the first thought was to give chase, have a merry fox hunt in the morning fog, albeit without horse or hound, when stumbling after the fox in all their hurry and surprise and mortification was a unit of the North Carolinas still lost at the end of the long and shot-filled night, as much dismayed as the Federals were to have gotten so lost in the confusion and so waylaid by the smell of coffee.

All the men stood aghast and unready in the moving cloud of mist and smoke, some with steaming cups, some with rifles. Mike had time to notice the rent at the knee of one Carolina boy's trousers, and the freckles that ran over his nose, had time to observe that everything was gray and brown in the mist, like the figures in photographs, that they all stood as still as the figures in photographs, posed with their weapons and their cocked hats and their startled staring faces. The only color was the red glow of the fire, and the red memory of the red fox like a splash of blood across the clearing.

Then to the left through the trees came the renewed boom of artillery, and bugle calls, and without a word the photographs dissolved and no one who had been there was there, and Mike was running back to where he'd left the Chancellor House.

It was battle he was in, the Lands of Badb, more confusing and disorderly than he'd ever thought, officers screaming orders none could follow, dead mules lying in the road, a dead horse *smoldering*, for God's sake, the bombarded topless trees like giant tombstones in the pale moving mist, the tang of gunpowder sharp as a bayonet in his throat, and up ahead, there was that stately building, broad and dignified, its ranked columns white in the mist. And to Mike the pale white glow of the sun rising behind it put a dome on the roof.

Then a cannonade bloomed behind him, knocking him forward in a hail of dust. He stumbled, his eyes on the house looming before him that looked, to his closing eyes, like the Capitol. And, "Jesus, Mairhe," thought he as he fell, "what have I done?"

5

"HOLY GOD, IT'S a bloodbath," Dooley moaned, all dismayed.

The faces around Finn with the newspaper were grim and grave, for none could believe that bloody eejit Hooker had actually lost. Lost! With superior arms and armies he had lost against Lee.

"Lincoln will eat him for supper," Finn said, turning the cheap pages with fingers black with newsprint. "But none of our boys in the casualty lists, thank the devil. D'you suppose your brother was in the fighting at all, Mairhe?"

"He's all right," said I. "I'm going to get him out before the next big battle. He wants out. Mark me."

"Mark her?" O'Callahan quirked a brow. "What d'you know about getting a man sprung from the Army's clutches?"

I cleared dishes into a basin. "I know what I know. He enlisted, he can get out if he wants."

"Mairhe," Dooley warned. "He enlisted, and that means he wants to fight."

"I will get him out, I say. I've an appointment to do so."

"And why'd you say he wants out, Mairhe? Tell us that?"

"I know what I know!"

The men at the Shinny passed a doubtful look around, but I didn't heed it. I'd not give up the only dream I had. I'd no other way to survive the worst thing that ever befell me.

"But Mairhe, this looks like an earnest offensive, now, and the Army will follow Lee—"

"I won't hear it!"

While the Shinny men pored over the casualty lists in the paper, I ran back through the kitchen to the alley for air. I didn't stop there but kept running on out into the main streets into the steady traffic of ambulances. I walked the side of the street, head down to pick my way across the planks that crossed the worst mud, and always at my shoulder, at the corner of my eye, were the wagons of wounded rolling through the streets from the steamer landings on the Potomac to the city hospitals. The air about me was filled with groans and cries for help, for water, for a doctor, for mother, and as the wagons lurched in the rutted road the screams would peak into such a weight of sound that it pressed down upon me ever harder until I broke anew into a run.

And when I raised my eyes, there in an open square was a great mortuary tent before me. I knew what it was, for the smell of the embalming cut through every other smell there ever was. The wagons and bearers that milled about that tent were dreadful to see, like flies swarming a dead cat in the gutter, and Capital Police holding back shrieking crowds of citizens in search of their boys. It was grotesque. This was what Hooker had done with the Army of the Potomac, turned it into so many wagons of customers for the mortuary men.

I knew Lincoln must be still at his hornpipe, striding down to his steamer and making his way up the Potomac to Hooker—who was retreating! Retreating in blockheaded confusion and still muttering about Richmond. And I on Lincoln's heels was busy with my own hornpipe, back and forth, skipping up and down with my hands crossed helpless behind me.

To the War Department I would go, and go again, and every day until I could secure my brother's discharge. He was an Irish boy, an alien, and had no business being in the war, and I told myself this as I ran through the crowded nurse-milling, ambulance-rattling streets. I told myself this as I made myself go up the steps full of officers and agitation, I told myself this as I closed my ears to the curses of men who told me to come back another time, didn't I know there'd just been a military calamity? until I was before Major Hanford and he looked up with pale blank eyes and spoke to me:

"Today the President has signed the Alien Conscription Act. Your brother would be drafted and bound to go now even if he hadn't already signed up. Of course, if you can find three hundred dollars for a substitute, and return the hundred-dollar bounty he took for signing up, you can buy him out. But I don't suppose an Irish girl like yourself can manage that sum?" He tapped his papers together.

"I thank you, sir. Where shall I bring the money whenever I've got it?"

Major Hanford laughed through his nose. "Oh, come back here and I'll tell you what to do with it. If you get it."

And with never giving him the satisfaction of making a poor Irish girl weep, I left his office and fought my way down the crowded stairs. My hands were cold as winter's ice, and my mind was a confusion of trying to clutch at so many threads at once. Four hundred dollars! Holy God, what a fortune!

But I could earn money. I had lace. I could make more. I could cast it as a net to bring Mike back in, as a lifeline, as reins. With one thread I could save my brother.

And so did I dance faster and faster, all alone to save his life. I was a spider, I was a spinner, I was the ropemaker's mother and the weaver's daughter, I was the weaverbird and the silkworm, plying thread to thread. I was the kite flyer and the fisherman, pulling out the thread to pull my brother in with. The lace pooled about my feet.

When I dreamed my brother marching in April, I wove him a banner to follow home. When I dreamed my brother lifting a wounded friend in May, I wove him a bandage to hold back the blood. When I dreamed my brother swimming in the hot June, I wove a net to bring him back to land.

And all the while was Lincoln dancing faster and faster too, back and forth, up and down the Potomac on his little steamer to confer with disgraced Hooker and say: Do you see that Lee is invading the North, sir? Do you see what the rebel is doing? Will you not take this army I have given you and *fight* against him, sir?

Hooker, still addled from Chancellorsville, could not attack the rebel general, but wondered to Lincoln if he shouldn't instead invade Richmond. The music came faster and faster at this point, and Lincoln was dancing aboard the *Carrie Martin* like the maddest sailor ever was. Then at last did Lincoln replace General Hooker with General Meade, and then his hornpipe was done.

Meade led the army to chase after Lee. The rebs were in Pennsylvania, where there lay a town called Gettysburg, and it was all woe to me then. For my hornpipe wasn't over yet.

6

I DREAMED I was an old, old woman, that my sight was dim and my hands spotted brown and knotted with veins. My voice shook like water shakes when the cold wind blows across it, my back was as bent as a mountain, and my hair as white as a dead moth's wing. All alone I sat in a chair in a darkened room, and the world was dark around me, and my age was upon me like a heavy, hurting cloak, but all sounds were present and strong as I tipped my paper ear to the world.

I heard the sound of men laughing before battle.

I heard the sound of blood dripping into a pan, and a doctor's footsteps walking away.

I heard the sound of paper tearing, a mother opening the letter that bears news of her son's death.

And I rocked and rocked in my chair all alone, hearing the three sounds of sorrow.

7

THIS IS THE way it happened on July 1, 1863, or so the story goes:

Rebel soldiers, having trudged all the way up

into Pennsylvania from their bean farms and their turpentine stills and their slow-river piers, and having had poor equipment to begin with (having but an impromptu government to support them), were marching on bloody feet. The ragged hems of their butternut britches licked their bare ankles. Their toenails were blackened with Maryland mud that caked and hardened on the hot summer road.

But there were shoes, someone said, shoes in the town of Gettysburg. And so the rebs turned back south down Cashtown Road in the heat, while the Feds were coming up north in the heat, and when they ran into one another, didn't the town begin to cook? Couriers and outriders boiled back through their own forces sending word, sending for support even as the artillery were hurriedly trundled and rolled into position and the officers in the rear were standing in their stirrups and straining through their field glasses and asking—What the hell is going on up there?

For none of them had known precisely where the other was, for to be sure, America is a big country, big enough for two big armies to lose one another in. And the weather was hot, and the men were dreaming of their hometown holidays upcoming, the Fourth of July picnics and horse races, the boating parties and the berry pies, the watermelons and chicken, the peaches warm from the sunny tree, and the sweethearts sitting under a sunny tree.

And God, weren't they tired, and weren't their feet sore and their legs aching? And their bellies not full enough with bad spoiled food, and their eyes not rested enough with bad spoiled sleep? But to hell with it all, for the enemy was there, and fight they must, for the shells were already pounding the ground and shaking the bricks from the houses, and the townfolk of Gettysburg rushing about and gathering up their scattered children and dogs and leaving their pickling half done on the kitchen table, the jars still tapping together as they boiled in the kettle.

And Mike was there, wasn't he?

Washington City was beside itself with the fear and the fury, the fighting truly north of us now and the rebels on Northern ground. We in the Shinny that July 2 and 3 sat waiting for each new edition of the newspaper through the evening, and Finn, or O'Callahan, or Dooley, or anyone with reading would read it. We stood gathered at the bar, our glasses untouched and growing warm in our hands, the heat heavy upon us and our heads aching with the heat and the worry of it all.

And as I heard the reports of the fighting on Little Round Top, Cemetery Ridge, and the Peach Orchard, Mike leaned back against a tree, wiping his smoke-black face on his sleeve and fixing his bayonet, his eyes white in his blackened face. The pounding of shells scarce made him flinch, for it was the regular sound of a beating heart, the sound of a hundred and fifty thousand beating hearts beating in time.

His company was gathered in the woods to the south of town, each man readying for the next attack. Some squatted on their heels, others leaned on their elbows or stood against the humid trees. Some men checked and rechecked their ammunition, fingering the bullets in their cases and squinting downhill through the tattered leaves. Other men wrote hasty notes to their wives or mothers and passed them to the captain. Some only stared dreaming into space, and the sound of their dreaming was the sound of water running over the stones in the near creek, and the low laugh of a man to his friend, and the murmur of prayer from another.

"Gallagher, give us your canteen, I'm dry as dust," Mike said.

Gallagher slung it off his shoulder, and passed it. The distant sound of rebel yells came to them like birdsong as Mike drank.

"Gives me a right uneasy sensation, how they scream," Gallagher said. He tried to spit but couldn't. "God, I'd like to be back in Ireland now."

"Would you? I wouldn't."

"P'raps you don't remember, then, what a lovely place it is," Gallagher replied.

Mike tossed the canteen to his friend, and tipped his head back to see the reddening sky through the mingling, croosheening leaves.

"I remember it."

He thought to say more, but didn't speak aloud, for his ears were filled with the sounds he wanted to hear: of waves on rocks and sheep bleating across the valleys, of spades turning wet earth and salmon thrashing up a stream, of a bagpipe's drone and a linnet's sweet call, and the sound of a woman washing clothes in a river. A sound of Ireland was in his ears.

"I remember it," he said again. "But I wouldn't go back. I choose America. It's good here."

And I bowed my head to the bar, all a wasteland in my heart. How could he say it? All he'd ever known was Swampoodle, the capital's slum, the hot, fumy slum at the heart of America. Here where it was hot, and the mud was thick and stinking, and we'd known nothing but trouble all our days since reaching this place. How could he say he chose America? What had it shown him but how to soldier on a hot road?

"Jesus, it's hot, isn't it?" O'Callahan complained. He ran a finger under his collar and drained his glass. "Well, good night to you all gathered here."

"Go to bed, Mairhe, you're done in," Mrs. Dooley said. She laid a hand on my forehead, palm down, then back down, and brushed the hair back from my face.

I pushed myself away from the bar, pushed myself up the stairs and to my room at the top of the Shinny, there to fall on my bed into a dreamless sleep.

I wakened in the dark.

There were no dreams.

There was no dream of my brother but the sound of a gunshot fading from my mind. My dreaming had failed.

I shook the matches at my bedside, and scraped one alight. The corners of my room rose from the darkness, the rocking chair, the foot of my bed, the blanket box, and everywhere, on every surface and in baskets on the floor, lay the round wound balls of my lace, yards upon yards of it, stacked like bone-white cannonballs, like balls of ice, trailing their sad raveling ends.

How had I thought to weave a mile of lace? What was I thinking? I could not make things so by saying so, I could not spin a story and say it was the truth, I could not weave my way to my brother, I could not rope him like a horse and make him not be what he was. If I'd had all the money in the world, I could never have bought my brother out of the Army, for he had chosen to give his fighting heart to America.

I stood from my bed and reached for one end of lace, letting the ball drop and unwind, and draped the film about my shoulders and hair even as I grabbed another ball. And that fell too, to unroll on the floor as I wrapped myself in my own net, and another fell and another, and I turned and turned within my web, my shift white, my skin white, my hair as black as night, wrapped in the white, white web. I'd caught no one but myself.

The lace was good for nothing but bandages and winding cloths now. My brother was no more.

8

THE FOURTH OF July 1863 was celebrated throughout Washington. The cries and cheers and whoops of joy echoed from every building: Lee is whipped and on the run!

What mattered that the wounded from the first day of battle at Gettysburg were already rolling into the city at the train depots, the wagons howling with pain in the heat? What mattered that the men struggling in on their own feet looked like dead souls walking the streets? Women rushed from their doors with glasses of lemonade and plates of cake to feed the walking ghosts. At last, a glorious Union victory. Lee was whipped and on the run.

What mattered that the casualty lists, the printers' ink still wet and smearing like blood on the hands, bore the names of entire companies, whole regiments, the populations of towns? What mattered that fifty thousand names were on those lists? Lee was whipped and on the run.

Mrs. Dooley sat me down when Mike's name was read from the sheet at the Shinny, and wrapped my hands around a mug of tea.

"There, acushla, cry on me." She rocked me against her breast and crooned a keening cradle song, though I didn't cry. I didn't cry.

"I wasn't there," I told her.

"No, of course you weren't."

"I wasn't with him."

Mrs. Dooley smoothed my hair. "No, how could you be?"

"I'm all in pieces, how'll I ever put myself together again?"

"What are you saying, acushla, my girl? Don't talk so."

I stared over Mrs. Dooley's broad shoulder, to see the Shinny boys standing around with nothing to say. None would meet my eyes, none would speak. Milky stroked Snatcher's fist-sized head, and Finn slowly shook his head, and Dooley put his head on his hands and sighed.

"Raise a glass now, boys," said O'Callahan, and cleared his throat. "To Michael Mehan. *Slainte*."

"Slainte," said they all together.

And I opened the door and went out in search of my brother's death.

I staggered along the streets as stricken as the walking soldiers, and walked staring and stumbling down one street and then another until I was on North Capitol Street, and heading down it in the stream of ambulances, nurses, and wagons toward the Capitol. And there, as in a dream, I found Mr. Walt waiting for me on the steps, and he led me up into the building that was a hospital today, as every building was.

Before my eyes in the Rotunda stretched row upon row of white cots, like snow-covered graves in a frosted boneyard, but gaudy with living blood. Above the cots keened the mingling, croosheening wails of the men, all undone and doomed, and echoing in the dome above.

"Come on, girl." Mr. Walt stepped all large and delicate to the first blood-dripping bed, and there kissed a cheek.

"How are you, son?"

The red-haired soldier there gripped Mr. Walt's

hand hard. His back arched. Above where his knees should have been was a spreading stain. "My sister's come, Doctor?" His voice was an Irish voice that made my heart faint. And then his back arched again and his cry of *"Ochone! Ochone!"* went through and through me like a cold red wind. Mike! Mike! Where is my brother?

"Your sister's here, son," Mr. Walt said to the raving man. "She's just arrived."

Mr. Whitman, the wildest largest-hearted dreamer of all, pointed and pointed at me until I *was* the man's sister and knelt by the bed and took the man's hot hand in my own.

"Sal? Is it you?"

"Here, macushla, m'darling," said I.

"Tell Ma I was brave," the soldier whispered to me.

"I will, macushla."

His eyes stared up. The red hair curled back from his brow, and a powder burn on his right cheek was wet and black. "And that I killed my share of rebs."

"I told her already, and she was glad to hear it but wants her boy home again. We sat last night over our sewing and spoke of our old times."

"And old Bren, he was there, Sal?"

"Sure. And we drank a health to you. *'Slainte!'* we said as we raised our glasses to you and called you our brave abu, our hero. And then one by one our neighbors stopped to drink *slainte* to you too."

"Not the MacReadys? They were never there too?" The man laughed, and stared hard at me.

I shrugged. "Sure and who but them? Didn't they always mean you well no matter what devil you did them?"

He laughed again and then cried again *"Ochone!"* And the red stain on his cover bloomed like a sudden rose and he died.

God send his spirit a dream of going home, a dream of stepping whole from the train in his Philadelphia, or his Trenton or his Albany, and seizing his laughing Ma in his arms and dancing her around. And she laughing and scolding and calling him her wicked spalpeen, her rascally rogue. Never would he have to say what house on the battlefield received him, what staircase running red he was carried up by the staggering stretcher men. There, where the fainting nurses bored holes in the floor to let the blood run out, where the surgeons carried their terrible saws from one man to another and parted man from limb—there was he parted from his dreams forever more.

"Mairhe," Mr. Walt said.

He took my hand to help me up, and we pulled the sheet over the soldier's face.

"I'll not see my brother again but in my own dreams."

"I think that's true, dear."

Mr. Walt moved down the ward, and was soon helping a nurse with a grisly chore. I stood over the shrouded soldier, and looked from him to the next and the next and the next, stretching away into the dimness. If I had my lace, I could join them one to another, bandaging their wounds with my work and binding their torn selves together.

I put my hand on the Irish soldier's head.

"Good-bye, macushla. Michael Mehan, good-bye."

Above my head was the old Capitol dome, round and fragile as the inside of an egg. And above that I knew to be the forming frame of the new dome stretching taller and reaching higher than ever before.

Would that old egg crack, and the broken boys down here be born from it and into the new? Did the Republic that labored so hard now plan to bring these boys with it? I strained to see upward in the poor light, up there where the mingling groans of the wounded soldiers resounded together, and I thought I heard the crack, so faint, only a crack.

THREE BRIGHTNESSES THAT GIVE HOPE IN TROUBLED TIMES

1

WHEN THE LONG day was over, and the parades of Independence Day were but echoes in our ears, I went down the steps of the Capitol. Below me on the lower stone steps was a seated figure, with a broad back and white hair, and I went to join him where it was cool in the twilight. Mr. Walt was bent close over one of his small notebooks, writing in it in pencil. I looked out on the Capitol grounds, where the statue for the top of the building lay in pieces, waiting its chance to ascend the dome. It put me in mind of the tower of St. Aloysius, and my Da, and how I'd have to tell him about Mike.

"I'd like to get my Da back to Ireland," I told Mr. Walt.

He looked up at me sideways, all weariness and care on his face. Or it may be it was only darkness. "Why is that?"

"He never liked it here. Never got over my Ma's dying, nor got over leaving home. Ireland's his all."

"Ah." Mr. Walt planted his elbows on his knees. "I know that emotion myself."

"And he might return to himself once he's back where he belongs."

"That may be. That may be. And where do you belong, Mairhe?"

"I don't know. I used to belong where my brother was, but not now."

"Can't you belong where Mairhe Mehan belongs?"

I didn't have an answer for him. I touched the notebook that gleamed faintly white in the fading light. "Why d'you always carry these about and write in them?"

"Oh, I make memoranda in them," he replied, turning the pages with his thumb. "What the boys want me to bring them, what letters to write for them. I describe what I see, my observations."

"What for?"

"For poems, Mairhe."

I was surprised. "Are you a poet, then, Mr. Walt?"

He pulled his beard. "I'm known for one or two small things."

"Not Irish, are you?"

"No, not Irish, Mairhe."

A company of soldiers marched past us where we sat on the steps in the gathering dark. The air was warm and damp, and in the distance was the sound of fireworks, perhaps gunshots— I think fireworks.

"Will you tell me a poem, then, Mr. Walt?"

"They're long things, mostly. Pages and pages."

"Give us a piece, then."

He turned to look up at me on my step, and he put his hand on mine. "Very well. Here's a piece for you: 'Listen dear son—listen America, daughter or son, It is a painful thing to love a man or woman to excess, and yet it satisfies, it is great, But there is something else very great, it makes the whole coincide, It, magnificent, beyond materials, with continuous hands sweeps and provides for all.' "

His face was obscure in the dark, but his white hair shone brightly, like a cloud after the sun has gone down.

"What does it mean?"

He stood up. "It will be plain to you soon enough, I hope."

And so he went down the steps and walked away from me, a poet with bright white hair. He disappeared into the darkness of the war-struck city, but his hair remained visible, a halo about his head, for a long, long time. And I, watching him, felt a restfulness occupy my heart.

At last I took myself off, and made my way back to Swampoodle and the Shinny. Along the way I saw a glimpse through a window here, and a view through an open door there, the people laughing and toasting one another for Independence Day and the great Union victory, or reclining on the front steps with a harmonica and loved ones singing, and all around the city an easeful, peaceful joy that the chance of union was yet preserved to us.

I walked among the Americans like a shadow of myself, and when I reached the thrown light of an open door, I stood in it and raised my face to the house where there was music from a piano and a noisy, puppyish chorus of "The Battle Hymn of the Republic." And laughter came with the music, and high girl voices and a father's low rumble, and a woman came to the front door in a blue dress, looking back over her shoulder as she came and speaking to the inside of the house where the gaslight burned bright in the wallpapered hall.

Then she turned to shut the door and saw me standing there in the light at the bottom of her steps, and she smiled at me.

"Happy Fourth of July," said she as she made to shut the door.

"Same to you, missus," said I.

She paused, and looked at me kindly. "What's your name?"

I wove my fingers together. *Mary*, I wanted to say. *Mary*. But I hesitated too long, and with another smile she nodded and said, "Well, good night, then."

So I took the crooked ways and the narrow ways to the Shinny, and when I walked in, all was strange to me though so familiar: O'Callahan and Finn arguing over a newspaper, Leary and Dooley leaning across the bar toward one another to share some wisdom, Milky feeding Snatcher sausage scraps from his plate, and all the other men with their old clothes and their new opinions, with Mrs. Dooley moving big and homely among them. I knew them all, but in a day they had become distant from me, and their voices foreign to my ear.

As I entered, first one man and then another noticed me, and gave me a nod or a smile, and Mrs. Dooley whispered to me that I should eat something, and then go upstairs, and not to bother with work at all for couldn't I see she could manage, poor lovey? And I embraced her kind self hard, and went away from them all to my room.

Their Irish voices murmured me to sleep.

2

I DREAMED I was on a ship, and the ship was bound for Galway. I leaned my elbows on the taffrail and looked over the stern at the waves racing beside us in our wake, how they spun white lace at their tops and dissolved on the blacky deep, and above my head the shrouds and rigging wove themselves together like lace against the sky. And the salt spray of the waves was cool on my face, and the warm wind was on my hair. My hands were empty.

But then I knew I'd gotten on the wrong ship, and looked around me for the captain or the pilot, for to beg them to change the course. Above me in the shrouds not a sailor stirred, no helmsman took the helm, nor was there another soul on the ship.

I ran to the bow, and looked down into the leaping waters that rose and fell away as the ship plunged ahead. The only sounds were the thump and clack of block and tackle against the masts, and the sigh and breath of the rigging, and the ship's bell telling, and the snap of the sails as the wind pushed me forward toward Ireland.

So did I look about me, and know there was none to help me. I looked forward again, where the bowsprit pointed like my own arm pointing ahead across the wide Atlantic.

And then of my own will standing in the bow did I turn the ship and turn the ship, until the bowsprit pointed back toward America.

3

IN THE MORNING, I gathered my lace together, great bags of it neatly rolled, and went to every milliner and mercer, every seamstress and dress-maker at work in the city, and turned my lace into greenbacks.

Fine stuff, they said, true Irish lace, handmade, not from a machine.

Lovely work this is, they said, beautifully made. Put your heart into it, didn't you?

Oh, they didn't know, they didn't know how I'd put my heart into it, they didn't know how I'd toiled on that lace, and what I'd tied it to, and what it had been meant to carry.

I went from one counter to another, watching them finger the lace with their long, hard fingers, watching them look at the lace with their hard-looking eyes, letting them take the measure against their arms and saying not a word as they hemmed and hawed and told me what they'd give for it. Some nine cents a yard. Some ten. One eleven. Most eight, for it was the war, dearie, money was tight and patriotic ladies were helping the war effort by wearing simple gowns, take it or leave it.

I never said a word to argue, only took what they offered for as much lace as they would buy, and then left, and went to another, and listened to the same story again through the long July day.

And when I had sold every yard, I had seventy-two dollars and thirty-eight cents, United States currency. I stood me on the sidewalk outside St. Aloysius and looked at the money in my hands. Enough. It was enough. The setting sun turned the greenbacks to gold in my hand, and the stretcher men coming in and out of the church paused to look upon me and quiz me with their looks.

I raised my eyes to the church. I'd not stepped foot in it for a year, not since the first wounded man had been brought in. I stuffed the money into my pockets and went in.

The adornments of the church were a balm to my eyes, the paintings on the walls and in the chapels, the holy scenes and the saints' lives, and the flickering lights at the altar put a soft bright seal of starlight on the beds and cots of wounded soldiers that filled the aisles and chapels. Stepping light and strong as a boxer from one bed to the next was my Da, his hair white in the candleglow.

I watched as he bent to one soldier, and then rose and spoke with an aproned nurse, and she patted his arm and nodded twice, and pointed him toward another man in another cot.

"Mairhe, it's good to see you." Father Wiget came from the shadows of a chapel behind me.

"Our Michael is dead."

"God rest his soul. Did it take that much to bring you to your Da, Mairhe?"

"Yes." I bowed my head to him, and he blessed me, and my tears came at last.

So he took me to my Da, and without a question my Da put his arms about me and held me close, and I told him about our Michael, and how he'd died in the fighting at Gettysburg, and my Da said he'd always known it would be so. For he was a Mehan, wasn't he, and wasn't he raised to be a fighter?

"Like you, my girl. Like you."

"I'm not a fighter," said I.

"You are, though. You're a Mehan, an Irishwoman."

I caught my tears at that, and pulled forth the money from my pockets. "Ireland, Da. Here it is at last. I've brought passage home."

He touched the greenbacks with an unsteady hand. "God. God."

"You've dreamed of it long enough, Da. You can go home."

"God," he said again, and wiped a tear.

"I'll talk with Father Wiget. I know he can make arrangements for you. Are you well enough? You seem well now, Da. There's still cousins and all back in Sligo who can look out for you."

Da was shaking his head back and forth, holding both my monied hands in his. Then he looked up.

"Mairhe. You don't sound like a girl who's coming too."

"No. No."

From a cot nearby, a man laughed, and then coughed. The nurse at his side scolded him gently, and he laughed again, but softer. He was a broken man, but he would be put together and be whole again and he knew it and it sounded in his laugh. The man struggled to sit up on his cot, and held up his bandaged arm as though to say—see, already it's better, I'm going to be better. And the white bandage in the darkness was bright as a star, delicate as lace, strong as a dream. And so was the soldier.

And so was I.

Mary Mehan Awake

PROLOGUE

Mr. Spencer F. Baird
Smithsonian Institution, Washington

Dear Mr. Baird,

Mysterious powers have brought us safely through this Civil War, and the news from Appomattox is greeted with hurrahs and catcalls on every street. Even you must have left your bird skins and your cataloguing to add your voice to the clamor. Now we turn the page. We begin anew.

Allow me to remind you of your offer to me when we last met in Washington; that you would gladly do me any service in repayment for the pleasure my poems have given you. I recommend to you a young friend of mine, Mary Mehan, who has been in the wards in the capital these past two years, and who requires a change of position to restore her soul and her health (which are as exhausted and trampled as the country is). This is what I ask: get Mary Mehan a domestic position far away from the scenes of war. She has a sharp intelligence, and has learned to read very quickly. You will find her quiet and hard-working. I know as well as anyone that nursing remains to be done there, but Mary has done her part and more. You have a broad acquaintance that reaches to the distant corners of our bruised country. Send her away, Mr. Baird. Send her far away to some quiet and peaceful place.

I remain yours in friendship,

Walt Whitman
Brooklyn, April 10, 1865

Mr. Jasper Dorsett
Grace Harbor, New York

Dorsett:

Providence lands in your lap once again. If you're still searching for a suitable person to hire, I've found you one: an Irish girl called Mary Mehan. I've seen her and find her sensible and willing to work (if a little morose, like many of her native land). She should do nicely as a companion to your wife, an assistant in your work, and a help in the house. She's trained as a nurse, has been a barmaid and so is used to doing coarse and heavy work without complaint, and she can read passably well (that fellow Whitman it was that taught her). These strike me as just the right qualities for your factotum. Say you'll hire her and I'll send her on immediately.

The last specimens you sent me were excellent. Walton writes from Nebraska that he has several whooping cranes ready to ship, including three chicks. Now this war's over we should see new efforts to send out the Surveying Expeditions, and we'll have specimens rolling in on every train.

Write by return post to tell me what to do with this Irish girl.

Affectionately yours,

Spencer Baird
Smithsonian Institution, April 13, 1865

Mr. Walter Whitman
Brooklyn, New York

Dear Mr. Whitman,

Thank you for your letter guaranteeing the character of Mary Mehan. Provided she is as suitable as you say, I am more than happy to employ her. You beg me to be kind in remembering that she has endured as many of the horrors of war as any battlefield veteran, and has done more than her share of the work in this late action. I am honored, no less than obliged as a patriotic American, to shelter her for this reason. We already have one wounded chick here. We'll take another.

Yours very truly,

J. Dorsett
Grace Harbor, New York, April 16, 1865

Dear Mary,

We have worked it all out and the Jasper Dorsetts will take you. Be a good girl. Work hard. Try to please them and they will treat you kindly and fairly. It is a very small household, so you won't have to speak very much—no din and chorus of conversation, I think. You will be safe there. Write to me if you think you can.

Your friend,

Walt Whitman
Brooklyn, April 20, 1865

BOOK I

All these—all the meanness and agony
without end I sitting look out upon,
See, hear, and am silent.

—Walt Whitman, "I Sit and Look Out"

Gray Window

THE STREETS OF the capital were wet and smoking, as though a fire had just been put out by the straining pumpers and bucket carriers. A poet might say that the country had gone through a conflagration and left the sky the color of ash. A politician would say the country had prevailed against insurrection and soundly punished the rebels. Mourning doves huddled on the dripping telegraph wires. Below them, black-coated people stood elbow to elbow under a canopy of black umbrellas. The black horses with muffled hooves steamed under the rain with their heads hanging, and the wheels of the carriages hissed through pools of water. The capital was as gray as Mrs. Lincoln's veil.

In a doorway stood a tall, dark-haired girl. Her face was turned away as the funeral cortege moved past, and so she appeared not to notice the melancholy parade. She stood silently, with her head bowed, her face composed and quiet, almost seeming not to breathe, a still, pale figure like a statue carved on a tomb. Once in a while, she marked the procession of the President's cortege in the reflection of a nearby window or in the dull shimmer of the puddles near her feet, or caught a fractured glimpse through the spectacles of the man standing in front of her. Her name was Mary Mehan, and she could not look at things directly anymore.

She had seen Lincoln once or twice, riding down North Capitol Street or going into Willard's Hotel. That was before she had made herself stop looking at people. Now no one would look at him again. She didn't feel sorry about it. She didn't feel anything at all.

When the procession had passed and the crowd began to break apart, Mary reached for two bags by her side, and then made her way to the depot. The capital streets continued to seethe and steam around her, but she moved with the detachment of a sleepwalker. If the crowd jostled her, she simply moved on again without stopping. At last, she arrived at the station and waited. There was little noise, or little that reached her. She stood alone in the doorway, unnoticed, making no sound. Nobody spoke to her. She had asked her few friends not to see her off. She had no family to watch her go away. Her brother had died at Gettysburg. Her father had returned to Ireland a broken man. She had no one. She was alone.

At the correct time she boarded the correct train, and did not notice the hand the porter offered her as she climbed into the carriage. Her thoughts were in shadow.

On the train she sat by a gray window. The locomotive jerked once, pushing her gently backward as the train began to move, taking her away from Washington. It gathered speed, flinging dark smoke back into the fog of the capital, where it fingered the mourners' black coats and mixed with the tears on stunned faces. Outside the city the damp countryside flashed by the window. Mary did not turn her head to watch the farmer's boys waving from a wagon as the train passed. She did not notice the dog chasing the train along a fence, a pantomime of barking beyond the window. The smear of coal smoke on the glass drained the countryside, and Mary noted only that the landscape was moving past, that it was day, that she was not in pain, not hungry or tired. Mary knew she was sitting by a gray window, but she did not look beyond it.

From time to time, as the train passed through sunlight and shadow, her reflection appeared before her on the glass. It was the face of a ghost surprised to be among the living. Sometimes the contrast of light was enough to show her the reflections of other people in the train, other refugees like her, veterans, the wounded. Mary recognized them by their startled faces, not by the remnants of uniforms or their crutches or slings. She recognized them by the way they sat so still, holding themselves so gently, so carefully against the rushing and rocking of the train. She recognized them by the way they sat with their hands quiet in their laps, empty at last of the tools of war. They recognized her by these same signs.

Maybe she had nursed some of these men on the train. It was possible; all soldiers looked alike when they lay in a hospital bed. Men had called her dear miss, and sweet Mary, and had wanted to hold her hand and dream of their own sweethearts at home. She had let them, and then covered them with sheets when they died of their wounds. And steadily, steadily, she had moved on to the next patient, and the next, and the next. They all looked alike in the hospital; they all died with the same finality. They died. That was their end.

Once there had been a time when she looked closely at them, and dreamed what their lives had been like before their meeting with an artillery blast in Virginia, or before Maryland dysentery drained them dry as last year's cornhusks. Once she had sat by their beds and dreamed along with them, dreamed what she might do after the war, dreamed of a sweetheart, a family, going west, being new.

But Mary had seen too many soldiers stop dreaming before her very eyes. She had seen the mortal fire grow dim in their faces and go out. She had carried away basins of blood, dripping bandages, fouled sheets, piles of left boots and right boots unmatched, never to be worn by their amputee owners again. And as she had done this, she had begun to feel as though every day she carried away some man's dream to throw on the middens pile. She had seen dreams cut off by the surgeons, coughed up by influenza, sweated away by typhus, bled white by wounds that would not heal, eaten away by gangrene.

This destruction had gone on around Mary for two years, and she was no longer convinced that dreams were the strong things she had once believed in, the things that could save a body's life or give that life meaning. They were too mortal, too fragile, too easily weakened and destroyed. And one day, Mary woke up. She realized that she no longer believed in dreams, and so told herself not to dream anymore, that it was foolish to dream, it was nothing but delusion, a weakness and a failing.

At the same time, she knew that her senses were enemies to her. Every day they attacked her with new assaults: the sight and smell of a wound that would not heal, the sound of muffled sobbing as a man soiled himself, the touch of a feverish hand on her wrist, the taste of foul air on her tongue. Every day they wounded her again.

But more than that, her senses were the messengers that brought the world into her mind, the whisperers of things that were and might be. A sick soldier might wish to show her the cherished, blood-stained photograph of his wife; Mary chose not to see it. Another man might wish to tell her about the green fields of Wisconsin; she made his words slip past her ears. Better, much better not to receive these things, for all these reasons. Mary could not bear it anymore.

The train rushed by trees swelling into leaf, and racketed around a bend and changed the angle of the weak sun. A cow pond held the pale sky in its bowl. The windows of a white farmhouse mirrored the trees in the farmhouse yard. In the train's gray window, Mary saw the reflection of the veteran seated in front of her. Tears ran down his face and into his whiskers as he watched the humble landscape hurry by. He cried silently, without movement.

Mary watched the soldier cry. She knew what made him weep: the war was over, and he was returning home to people who loved him, but they would never imagine what he had seen, and now he knew, now he suddenly understood, that he would have to live alone forever with those things he had seen. Alone forever.

In the reflection, their eyes met, and then, at the same time, they shifted their gazes away and stared through the pane of glass that separated them from the rest of America.

Oval Mirror

THE VILLAGE OF Grace Harbor rested upon the shores of Lake Ontario like a swimmer resting upon the beach, stretching itself and gazing into an oval mirror. The main street terminated at one end at the train station, and at the other end at the pier and the harbor. Passengers alighting from the New York Central Railroad cars were therefore greeted by a vista of the great lake spreading off into the horizon, and of the rising and falling boats that might ferry them there. In the depot waiting room, Mary watched the glimmer of lake light explore the ceiling; she could not see the boats.

Jasper Dorsett, naturalist, had sailed into that vista thirty years earlier, leaving behind a commission to West Point so that he could be bird and plant man in a survey expedition to the Great Lakes and the new Wisconsin Territory to the west of them. And then, leaving the survey and equipping himself with funds from home, Dorsett followed the flights of birds across Lake Superior into Canada. For fifteen years he crossed from Manitoba and Ontario to Minnesota and Wisconsin, collecting specimens to send to the universities of the east and later the Smithsonian, venturing farther north each time, living in all ways with the birds and plants he studied. Many times he went hungry rather than eat a rare bird just collected.

This was the man who was now driving his gig along Ontario Street, which met the main street of Grace Harbor at a right angle. As he turned the corner, Mary was standing at the window of the station waiting room, watching a robin in the street. Mary saw its beak open as it sang, but no sound reached her through the glass. Then the bird burst away in the next moment as the gig bowled up the street toward the station, and through the blur of spokes Mary saw the robin settle again and open its yellow mouth once more, puffing out its chest.

The gig stopped at the station. A man of middle age hopped down from the driving seat, wrapped the reins around the brake handle, and puffed out his chest. He tipped his head to one side, regarded the train station, and then hurried in.

"Say you're Mary Mehan. Do say so!" he sang out.

"I am Mary Mehan, sir," Mary replied.

The man cocked his head to the other side. "Giving satisfaction already! That's very good. So glad you could join us, and you say you can read, is that right? You don't look very strong! That Whitman fellow said you're strong."

"I am, sir, very strong."

"And have a good voice, too," Dorsett said. "Although you don't use it much, I'll guess. Here we go! Surprised to find your new employer fetching you from the station, eh? Our man is deaf and doesn't like to drive to meet strangers, poor fellow. Into the gig! That's it!"

And with a snap of the reins they were rolling down the street.

"You'll find our household very cozy!" he continued over the clattering of the wheels and hooves, and his voice faded and came back to Mary in jerks and starts. "Me. Mrs. Dorsett. Rose, the cook. And Henry—just as I mentioned. Deaf. The war. Artillery crew. Such a shame. So many losses . . ."

"Yes, sir," Mary agreed. She watched her hands, saw the shadows that fell across them from the branches of the trees arching over the road, and in this way spent the remainder of the short journey while Dorsett outlined her duties.

Mary was to assist his wife in matters pertaining to wardrobe, linens, and household management, and to read to her when asked and be company to her. When not wanted by Mrs. Dorsett, Mary was to assist him, primarily in his activities with his camera and photographic equipment, but also with the recording of descriptions of specimens, and the correspondence he carried out. For indeed, although no longer a naturalist with his shotgun and canoe, Dorsett was still a naturalist with his pocketbook and pen, and provided financial support to younger men now in the field, receiving shipments of specimens to be photographed, properly measured and described, mounted, and shipped to the Smithsonian.

"And of course, I'm not completely bound and tied to my study," he added. "I do get out—trying to photograph the creatures alive in their natural state, but it's hard! Problems of exposure time! Sudden movement! A challenge! But I'm at it! I'm at it!"

Mary tried to listen, knowing she must listen, but having no idea, really, what he was talking about. The landscape around her was the greatest extreme from what she had always known, the dirty alleys of the capital's Irish slum and the crowded hospital wards. But she could only look at it from the edges of her vision as the gig rattled along the road. Those were unleafed trees there, here was a stream slipping under a wooden bridge, and there a fallow field awaiting the plow. Jasper chirped at her side, as much a part of the landscape as the small brown birds bursting up from the bare branches of the chestnuts as the gig hurried on.

Mary couldn't always understand him. She couldn't hear him distinctly, just as she couldn't see clearly what the landscape showed her. She held herself as still and quiet and careful as she had on the train, until they pulled up a long drive to a rambling white house with spreading porches and green shutters. Beyond, Lake Ontario opened into the horizon. A cool strong breeze swept across Mary's face.

"How do you like our puddle?" Dorsett asked.

Mary was silent for a long moment, seeing only the dazzle and shimmer. "I have never seen a lake before."

The man drew the horse up in front of the house. He gaped at her. "Never seen a lake?"

"No, sir." And with an effort, Mary added, "Mr. Dorsett, I have always lived in the city."

"But—"

But then his gaze suddenly darted away as some wonderful sight caught his eye, and he called, "Diana, my dear," and threw aside the reins.

Mary saw a change come over his face and in this way knew how beautiful his wife was. Dorsett hopped down from the gig, calling eagerly.

"Look what I've brought you. The new girl. Mary, this is Mrs. Dorsett."

Diana Dorsett had been walking. She wore a long white wool coat against the breeze, and the hem of her white dress was stained with mud and new grass. She held a white feather, and drew it first through one hand, and then the other, letting it twine through her bare fingers. The wind had put color into her face and pulled a lock of blond hair from beneath her hat.

"Welcome," she said to Mary, slowly twining the feather through her hands. "My husband has been so anxious for your arrival. So have I. We hope you'll be very . . . content with us."

"Thank you, Mrs. Dorsett."

"How was your journey? Were you comfortable?"

"Thank you, ma'am. I had no trouble."

Mrs. Dorsett turned to her husband and put a hand on his arm. "Darling, speaking of trouble, I'm afraid Nanuk has done it again. He caught a sparrow and the poor creature is suffering. I put it in the stable."

"I'll mend it, I'll mend it!" Dorsett said. "Where was his bell? How I let you talk me into keeping a cat I'll never know."

"Because you're the kindest of men, my dear."

Dorsett blushed with pleasure. "Impossible. I'm as cruel and hard as ice!"

"Of course you are," his wife laughed. "Now, shouldn't you have a look at that poor bird?"

And then they were both gone, moving across the lawn toward the side of the house. Mary climbed down from the gig and stood by the horse's head, looking up at the white house and then away. The horse put his head down to rub his fetlock. The door of the house opened.

"Oh, there they've left you—"

Mary looked up in time to glimpse an immensely fat woman framed in the doorway before the door slammed shut again. The place was utterly silent. She stood still, breathing quietly, waiting, while two swallows dove across her vision and flashed away. The door opened again.

"Come in, come in!" The fat woman beckoned to Mary, sneezed, and beckoned again. "Come in! It's freezing cold! Henry's coming for the horse, just leave it. Leave your bag."

So Mary walked into the house, and the woman

stepped aside, sneezing again before shutting the door.

"I'm the cook. Rose. Let me show you your room."

Rose turned and gathered her heavy skirts to lead the way up the broad stairs, and through a window Mary saw a young man walk from the side of the house to the gig and lead the horse away.

"It's a large place, but you'll find the work none too hard," the cook said as she labored up the stairs. "Mrs. Dorsett dreams the day away. Mr. Dorsett met her up in Canada; her father was the director of the Hudson's Bay Company at Fort York, and I can't even imagine what a specimen of remoteness that is. So she seems to be quite content all on her own; they don't entertain much unless it's one of those explorer men coming with their smelly packages and bones and talking till all hours with Mr. Dorsett, and they're not particular, just glad for a warm bed and good food. And no children, of course, which is a pity for them but makes for an easier house. But the dusting!" Rose paused on the landing, waiting for Mary. On a table at the turn of the stairs was a bell jar with a stuffed white owl inside.

Mary looked through the glass at the owl as Rose caught her breath. The round marble eyes glinted in the filtered light of the stairway. "I don't mind the hard work," Mary told the cook. "I'm willing to work."

"No, of course you are. I'm sure you're a good girl. Irish, are you?"

"Yes, ma'am."

"Never had an Irish girl here before. German girls, now they're good hard workers." And so Rose continued upward, still talking, leading Mary past racks of antlers mounted on the walls, framed maps, engravings and paintings of birds and ferns and flowers. Chips and splinters of light slid off specimen cases filled with stuffed birds as Mary walked. Light fell from the prisms of the chandelier poised high above the stairwell and rolled around the glass globes of the lamps.

Mary knew she was a stranger among these things, a specimen more odd and unusual than any freakish natural thing in the cases, without benefit of shell or claws or spiny quills or other protection. She ascended the staircase like a bubble, drifting, fragile, separate. She knew these people had no idea how separate from them she was. At the top of the stairs, a large oval window let in a bright, shifting illumination that made her blink.

Mary's steps faltered as she passed before the window. She looked out for a moment at the brilliant lake, and then turned. On the wall opposite, a large oval mirror echoed the landing and the view.

The landing and all its birds and prints and horns were washed in the glimmering light of Lake Ontario. And against the light, Mary saw herself in dusky silhouette, like a swimmer in deep water looking toward the surface.

The Lens

THE HOME OF Jasper and Diana Dorsett occupied the center of a wide, sloping lawn, the way a vase of flowers occupies a table. It sprawled, just as a loose arrangement of wildflowers sprawls, with a porch trailing along one side, a glasshouse sticking out on another, and a turret poking up through the middle like a spike of foxglove.

The interior of the house was less a field-picked bouquet than a botanical garden, the contents ordered in ranks, everything labeled and catalogued. Jasper Dorsett had filled this cabinet of wonders to overflowing with the magnificent specimens of the natural world—fossils, articulated skeletons, shells and pressed ferns, mounted birds and mammals in artful poses, bowls of polished chestnuts, butterflies, petrified bracket fungi, glittering crystals and minerals, a glass conservatory with its cage of cheeping finches nestled among the tropicals—each specimen more compelling in its perfection than the last. *Lagopus lagopus* in its winter white feathers sat beside the pressed flowers of *Cypripedium reginae*, quartz turned sunlight into rainbows to fall over shells of the angel wing, the northern moon snail, and the cross-barred venus.

And shedding more light over it all was the spirit of Diana Dorsett. Her image, in photograph after photograph, gazed upon her husband's collections, and regarded itself in the reflections of countless mirrors.

To the south of the white, rambling house was the road, and endless apple orchards stretching across the flat, fertile plain of the Ontario basin. At the west of the house was a garden folly, a rustic gazebo of peeled logs and grapevine trellises, which in summer would be greenly overgrown with Dutchman's-pipe and flaming honeysuckle. To the north lay the lake, giving back to the sky every drop of light that rained down on it. At the edge of the lake was a green-gabled boat house, spangled with reflections.

And east of the Dorsett house, following the gravel drive, was a carriage house with a stable, home to the bay mare who pulled the family gig, and home to the gig itself. Around the carriage house were vegetable gardens and cold frames, a beehive, a paddock, a yard for chickens. On the second floor of this carriage house, its window giving onto the orchards and the lake, was a small apartment.

The tenant of this apartment was Henry Till, the son of Grace Harbor's Methodist cleric. Educated, musical, a lover of baseball and horses, Henry had laid his sheet music down on his mother's piano in 1861 and traveled into the land of war.

For two years Henry served on an artillery crew, priming and loading the cannon, ready with the next ball even as the giant guns fired. Because the artillery was always the focus of the enemy's own guns, Henry had seen one companion after another shelled to pieces before his eyes, seen the artillery horses' legs blown off amid fountains of dirt. The horses' screams and the men's screams grew fainter every day while the cannons fired again and again by Henry's ears. Whether he lost his hearing from the roar of the guns or from an act of will to shut out the screams, lose his hearing he did. Henry had loved music, but he gave it up at Gettysburg.

And now, when he should have been enrolled at

Columbia College, he worked for Jasper and Diana Dorsett. He minded the horse, kept the gardens and grounds, helped Rose with heavy housework, and lived in silence above the carriage house.

Rose kept a slate and chalk in the kitchen, and she explained their use to Mary when their tour of the house brought them there. "Henry can talk, but he won't, poor lamb, so we write our notes to each other here. You know your letters, do you?"

Mary nodded. "Yes, Miss Rose."

"There, that's fine, then. You'll be able to speak with him, too." Rose raised the lid of a steaming pot on the stove. She stirred it, sniffed. "Can't smell a thing with this stuffiness of mine. How does it smell to you?"

Mary breathed in. She could smell nothing. Nothing. "I'm sure it's fine," she hazarded.

One of the bells above the hall door bounced and clanged. Rose clapped the lid back on the pot and bustled Mary around. "There's Mr. Dorsett wanting you now. Off you go."

After the bright kitchen the hallway was dark, so dark that Mary had to wait for her eyes to grow accustomed to the dimness. One by one, the strange objects defined themselves to her, their shapes and sizes growing clear, and she began to move forward. The hallway through the center of the house was still dim, but she could see her way well enough, and soon came to Dorsett's study, adjacent to the glasshouse.

Her employer sat hunched over his desk, peering at something on the blotter through a magnifying glass. Without looking up at Mary's knock, Dorsett waved her in, toward the desk. Nearby, birds chirped and cheeped faintly.

"See here, this is very fine," Dorsett said.

Cautiously, Mary moved to the desk and took the lens he held out to her. Through it she looked down at the smooth brown rock sitting on his desk and, bringing the lens closer, brought the impression of a feather into focus.

"Indiana limestone—wonderful what we find in it. Lovely, isn't it?"

Mary studied the fossil. The barbs running out from the central quill lay flat against each other, perfectly parallel, tapering out to the tip, except in one spot where some force had separated them into a vee. Even a faint trace of wispy down at the bottom of the feather was etched into the stone. It was photographic, a portrait of any and all feathers Mary had ever seen. She nodded her agreement.

"Feathers are a part of the bird's skin, much like hair on mammals and scales on fishes. But we can't fly with our hair! Too bad, too! I believe this one is from a bird of the wren family," Dorsett said, and began pulling books from the stacks around him, turning to the engraved pictures, humming to himself, seeming to forget Mary standing there.

Mary continued to gaze through the magnifying glass at the fossil, and then looked at the fine surrounding grain of the limestone, and then brought the palm of her own hand under the lens. It jumped up at her, large and startling. She turned her hand over, examined the backs of her knuckles, the white moons of her fingernails. And then, her heart beginning to beat faster, Mary turned the lens on her wrist, seeing in full detail the whiteness of her sleeve, the threads that held the buttons in place, the warp and weave of the fabric, the fine dark hair on the back of her arm. The lens made it all so sharp and clear.

"So, you're settled in, I hope? Everything comfortable?"

Mary put the lens down abruptly, and the world around her retreated into smallness and vagueness again. "Yes, sir. I know I will be very happy here."

"*Hmm.*" The man tipped his head to one side. "You don't look very happy now."

"No, sir." Mary could hardly hear her own voice.

"I know you've had a difficult time of it." He paused, waiting for her to speak, but she did not speak. "A terrible time. You must have suffered greatly to see so much suffering."

The finches in the next room cheeped and twittered. Mary found herself wanting to pick up the lens again, but put her hands behind her back instead. A sudden choking pressed in on her chest. She had seen so many terrible things. Too many. She could not speak of it.

"Mary, come with me."

With a jerk, Dorsett hopped up from his chair and opened the glass doors behind his desk. He led the way through the glasshouse and outside. Mary followed him across the lawn without speaking, passing the rustic summerhouse toward the line of trees that reached down to join the lakefront. An old stone wall lay tumbled among the trees, and Dorsett made his way along this, pausing now and then to brush aside dead leaves with his boot. "Here's one. I knew they were out. Mary, come have a look."

The flower Jasper Dorsett exposed to the sun was starry white, its petals quivering in the breeze. "*Sanguinaria canadensis*. Bloodroot," he said, reaching down and tugging the flower from the stem. He held it aloft for Mary to examine.

From the broken stem, one drop of blood-red sap welled out and fell onto Dorsett's outstretched hand, its curve magnifying the lines of his palm like a lens. Another spilled out and pooled with the first, doubling the lens. Mary looked at it, feeling tears well in her eyes at the same rate.

Dorsett saw her tears and cleared his throat gruffly. "The Indians I knew in Canada use it for dye, and sometimes to ward off insects." His palm held the gleaming puddle of red sap until he tipped his hand, and it spilled out onto the dead leaves.

"Forgive a scientist for making clumsy metaphors, my dear girl," he said in a gentle voice. "But that is the only blood you'll see here. I promise you. You're through with that now."

Overhead, a line of geese in formation headed out across Lake Ontario, heading for the north. Dorsett turned his face to the sky, following the birds' progress. "Do you hear them?" he asked.

Mary shook her head.

"You will," Jasper said. "Now, let us go in. We have work to do."

Glass Plate

JASPER DORSETT OWNED several cameras, and had outfitted a spacious darkroom. In this darkroom, illuminated by the yellow light of two kerosene lamps with amber glass shades, were row upon row of tools and equipment: the developing-out tanks; the great bottles of collodion, ferrous sulphate developer, and cyanide fixer; the glass plate holders and sensitizing baths; wooden frames and presses for smoothing and drying the prints.

And in a corner of the conservatory, off of which the darkroom was sited, was an impromptu studio: a regal chair upholstered in blue velvet, draperies on rods, several tall tables, the largest of Jasper's box cameras on a tripod. Perched on one of the tables was a stuffed gull, mounted with wings outstretched. Dorsett had been experimenting with techniques for the most lifelike photographs of birds. It was a great frustration to him, however, that he was compelled to take the images of dead birds. It was true that the great Audubon had shot his birds and wired them onto a frame in natural poses in order to render the most vital, living representation, but Jasper Dorsett had been made impatient and urgent by the advances of science.

"The process is thus: the collodion is a solution of sulphuric and nitric acids," Dorsett explained, raising one of the lamps to shed light on the darkroom shelves. "We pour the collodion across a plate of glass, and then sensitize it with silver nitrate, rendering the glass susceptible to light. When this plate is exposed to rays of light coming through a lens, the photochemical reaction etches the collodion and silver into a negative image of what the lens sees. Marvelous! Then, using such a plate, sensitized albumen paper can be likewise exposed, forming a positive print, a photograph."

He had been experimenting outdoors, he continued, trying to photograph the birds as they lived and breathed, fed their young, gave voice. But at least ten seconds of perfect stillness was required for a sharp and distinct image—and ten seconds were more than most birds cared to wait. Around the studio and darkroom was scattered the evidence of his experiments: dozens of glass plates, showing in negative the blurred outlines of wrens, robins, gulls, ducks.

Mary's first task was to collect these failures, remove them to the darkroom, and recapture the silver. Jasper's instructions were clear, and Mary understood him well, and so within two hours of arriving at the Dorsett home, Mary was alone in the darkroom, dipping glass plates into a chemical bath to leach out the silver and clean the plates.

It was perfect work for her, methodical and solitary. She took comfort in the darkness of the room, the orderly rows of bottles with their printed labels. The lamps hissed quietly. One by one, Mary examined the glass plates, peering in the amber light at the shadowy figures on the glass. They were all birds, more birds than she knew names for. Some of the plates showed a collection of blurs, the sudden rushing movement of a flock rising into the air. Some plates showed a crow, distinct except for the head, which might be in two or three poses at once, or the fuzzy outline of wings that seemed to shake and rustle even as she looked at them.

With each plate she looked longer, lingered over

the clear and opaque forms. This is a very small bird, she would say to herself as she looked at a plate. Or, this bird is holding a grasshopper in its mouth. This one is looking into its nest. Even blurred and imperfect, the images showed her clearly what the birds were doing. It amazed her that she could observe these creatures from such a distance, so long after their quick movements had been frozen onto the glass.

After examining each negative, Mary lowered the plate on a glass rack into the tank, washing it gently back and forth, until the plate was clean and clear when she removed it. When she had cleaned and rinsed the plates, she set them to dry on a wooden rack. She moved a lamp nearer, and held up one plate by its edges to gaze through it. The images she had seen on it were completely erased. When the rack was filled, she went out into the studio to search for more negatives, and repeated the process: washing, clearing, erasing. The failures disappeared one by one. The cloudy, confused images were washed away.

She dried the plates and stacked them on a corner of the darkroom table, and then stood at the open door of Dorsett's study. "I've cleaned all the bad plates, sir."

He turned and blinked at her. "All of them?"

"Yes, sir. I believe I found them all."

"Well, now that's very good. Very good. Find your way about the darkroom all right?"

"Yes, sir."

"Now that you've erased the images, care to see how they're made? Here, start with first principles," he exclaimed, and swooping into the conservatory, he flung up the black drape on the back of the large camera. "Look through there."

Mary did as she was told, stooping to put her head under the drape. She heard Dorsett's footsteps as he crossed the room, and as she aligned her eye with the viewpiece, she saw the blue velvet chair and Dorsett seated on it. He explained the details of wet plate photography and printing, and Mary found that by moving the front face of the camera forward or back, she could bring nearer things into focus, or farther things. She could see the nap of the velvet on the chair, the folds of the drapes, the light slanting down through the glass roof. She focused on Dorsett as he spoke, and for the first time noticed how beaky his nose was, how bright his eyes, how quick and birdlike his movements. She could see him clearly through the camera, his homeliness, his quick smile.

At the sound of a knock he darted up from the chair and disappeared from the view of the camera.

Mary withdrew from under the drape, turning to see who had beckoned. Through the open door to the study, she saw Dorsett engaged with Henry, the young man she had seen leading away the gig. They passed a notebook back and forth across a desk, each writing in it in turn. Mary moved closer for a better view. Their conversation was entirely silent: if the glass doors had been closed and she watching through them, she could not have been more cut off from them.

Dorsett left his study, going out the door into the hallway, and Henry was left in the room. Mary was surprised that he did not leave right away. Instead, he stood before a bookcase, and took down a book and began to leaf through it slowly. His face was turned in profile to Mary, and she could see that he had not noticed her standing there in the glasshouse.

Mary watched him through the doorway as he read through several pages, and as she looked at him she thought, He was a soldier, he was in the war, he knows what I know. He is like me. Then, realizing that she was spying on him, she moved backward suddenly and caught her skirt on the corner of a glass plate perched at the edge of a table. It crashed to the tile floor, making the finches burst into frightened, noisy chaos in their cage.

Aghast, Mary looked at Henry. But he had not heard the glass breaking. He could not have heard it. In the silence, Mary listened to the beat of her heart grow calmer. As Henry continued to read in Dorsett's study, Mary left the glasshouse by the outside door and saw the new green grass of the lawn bending in the breeze, saw the water moving on the lake, saw the sky.

BOOK II

When late I sang sad was my voice,
Sad were the shows around me with deafening noises of hatred and smoke of war;
In the midst of the conflict, the heroes, I stood,
Or pass'd with slow step through the wounded and dying.

But now I sing not war . . .

—Walt Whitman, "The Return of the Heroes"

Rounds and Shells

THE HOME OF a wealthy man engrossed in studious pursuits, and a wife accustomed from childhood to solitude and few luxuries, is not a home that expects constant toil from its servants. There was no busy entertaining, no fussing about trivial matters, no fits of melodrama. The house was easy and undemanding, the doors and windows open to the spring air from the lake. If a dead leaf blew in, it was found soon enough. Breezes made themselves at home, making the prisms on the chandeliers sway and chime, nudging the doors of the rooms a little wider. It was Diana Dorsett who pushed out the casements and opened the doors, craving the cool air that was familiar to her from her girlhood in Canada. Only Rose grumbled from time to time about a chill, complaining that she would fall victim to another cold. The white cat, Nanuk, padded about the house and went in and out through the windows with the breeze.

Very shortly after Mary arrived, Rose turned over the shopping to her, claiming that she had never favored riding in the open gig at the mercy of the wind. So every morning, after the breakfast chores had been completed, Mary went to the carriage house, where Henry would have the gig ready. Then, with maybe a nod or a brief smile for greeting, the two would ride in silence to Grace Harbor.

Mary was glad that Henry did not speak. Making her rounds in the hospitals, she had listened for hours to soldiers telling her their griefs, their fears, and their broken promises, and she had used up all her powers of listening and responding. Knowing that Henry did not expect her to speak, that she did not have to reply to questions or make conversation, made her grateful to him. His silence allowed Mary to look around her or study the shopping list given to her by Rose. Sugar, she would read to herself, milk, butter, string. She would show Henry the list, and he would stop the gig at the appropriate shops and wait for her.

In the shops, Mary would name her needs to the clerks in a low voice, then count out the money or ask that the charges be put on the Dorsett account. If one of them should try to draw her out, she would reply quietly that yes, she worked for the Dorsetts; yes, she was Irish; and thank you, good-bye. Sometimes the clerks had to speak to her twice before she heard their questions. She hardly noticed or did not care that some people eyed her askance for being Irish—people had always held that against her. She did not hear the little boys mocking her accent as she left the post office.

If there were heavy items to be carried, Henry would come in with her to carry them, and with their errands complete, they would leave the town in as deep a silence as they had arrived at it, with the lake sparkling and glinting through the trees along the roadside.

Sometimes Mary wondered about Henry's deafness. She wondered how many explosions had gone off by his ears, how many times he had loaded the artillery with the heavy iron shells. How many rounds did it take to kill a man's hearing?

Mary gradually noticed that on these rides Henry watched the bay mare, and that when the horse swiveled an ear to the right or the left, Henry would glance that way, and so Mary would glance that way, too. She would then see a crow flapping over the bright sheet of the lake, or the yellow drooping fingers of a willow stirring in the wind, or the white tail of a deer breaking away through the orchards at the approach of the gig.

"I don't hear them either," she said one morning as Henry turned the horse up the drive to the house.

Mary thought she should write it for him to read, that she would tell him that. But she didn't, and when she climbed down at the gravel path to the kitchen door, she simply watched him drive on to the stable, and then went inside.

Rose was bending over, peering into the oven. The cook raised herself heavily as Mary put the day's shopping on the table.

"Oh, you're back—did that package come that Mr. Dorsett was so anxious for?"

"There was a crate at the station," Mary replied. "Henry will bring it in."

"Run and tell Mr. Dorsett, he's been asking."

Mary unbuttoned her coat. "Is he in his study?"

"Study?" Rose looked at her with an expression of surprise on her round red face. "They're in the music room—don't you hear that racket they're making?"

Slowly, Mary turned to the door. "I think I do," she began.

"Go on, go on. I'll tell Henry to take it in there."

Mary followed the passage through the house.

From a distance came a chord on the piano, and then faint laughter like an echo. She paused, turning her head to catch another sound. The music began again, finding its way to her uncertainly like a lamp approaching through smoke. Mary followed it.

The door of the music room stood open. Diana Dorsett was seated at the piano, smiling up at her husband, who stood at her side.

"Not that melancholy Chopin, my love," the man said. "Play something we can sing to."

"Very well, darling."

Diana brought her hands to the piano and began to sing, and after a moment, Dorsett began the same song in a round. Their voices rose together, chasing one another like two birds around the room.

Mary stood in the doorway, watching them sing. She saw how they looked at each other, how Dorsett's hand rested so tenderly on his wife's shoulder, how Diana's fingers ran over the keys. Never in her life had she seen two people act as affectionately toward each other as these two, singing their round in the sunny room.

She turned away. Henry was carrying a box down the hallway toward her. Quickly, Mary knocked on the music room door and the music stopped in mid-song. The Dorsetts both turned to look at her.

"Excuse me, sir, the box you were waiting for is here," Mary said, stepping aside to let Henry into the room.

"Excellent!" Dorsett clapped his hands together. "Let's see what it contains, shall we?"

"I know what it contains," Diana laughed. She let her fingers touch the piano keys on each word: "Bird skins. Fossils. Dried moss . . ."

Henry took a pry-bar from his pocket and opened the crate. Diana winced as the nails squealed, but Dorsett put his hands in as soon as the lid was off, digging through the sawdust.

"From California," he said gleefully. "Henderson promised to send me—ahh, what have we here?"

Beaming, he drew out a large white shell with a pink lip. "A California conch, I imagine. Fine specimen."

"Let me take a look, darling." Diana spun lazily on the piano stool and reached for the shell. "Can I hear the ocean in it?"

She held it to her ear, smiled a dreamy smile, and held it out to Mary. "You try it, Mary."

Puzzled, Mary took the shell and put it against her ear. At first she heard nothing, but gradually she noticed a distant steady whispering, like water rushing in a stream, or wind blowing, or a fuse burning on an artillery piece.

She turned her gaze to Henry, but he was gone. She had not heard him leave.

WAVES

WHEN AN OBJECT begins to vibrate, the air beside it bends and vibrates as well, sending a wave through the air like a swell rolling across a lake. The wave may strike a sensitive receiver, which will resonate with the motion to transmit sound. The greater the wave, the harder the impact. Thus, a whispered voice caresses the ear like a ripple upon the lake. Steady thunderous explosions break upon the ear like a storm surge, destroying the shore.

Waves crested and spilled onto the sandy edge of Lake Ontario as though it were the drum of a giant ear, bearing the sounds of the sister lakes to the west, their dunes and whispering wild rice shores, news of broad blowing grasslands that thundered with shaggy herds, reports of the columbine nodding in landslide cracks among the Rocky Mountains, and from farther still, the Pacific, the Orient, the wide world.

Up in the Dorsett house, the sound of those waves came faintly to Mary. At first she had not noticed the sound at all. But if Henry entered her line of sight while she was working—if he came into the kitchen as she polished silver, or if she saw him working in the garden as she filled the seed dishes in the finches' cage—she listened, wondering what might be out there that he couldn't hear. His deafness reminded her that there were sounds. She listened for the waves she could see breaking on the shore. When Henry was in sight, she heard them, but just barely.

One morning, as they drove back from town, Mary was startled by a sudden sharp bird call that was so musical and piercing that she jerked around in the seat for a glimpse of the bird. Behind the gig, the road rolled backward. On either side, trees were leafing out, spreading a green May mist over the lane.

She sat forward again, and noticed Henry looking a question at her. Mary took the shopping list and a pencil from her basket and wrote, *A bird which I have never heard before.*

Henry shifted the reins to one hand so that he

could pick up the note and pencil. He wrote on his knee as the gig bounced along, *What was its call?*

It sang "a mel-o-deeeee!" wrote Mary.

He smiled and wrote, *Red-winged blackbird.*

Mary glanced at the roadside, listening for the blackbird again. "A mel-o-deee," she sang under her breath.

Only a few moments later, Henry pulled in the reins, and the bay slowed to a walk and then stopped. He opened his hand for the paper and pencil. Mary watched his hand as he wrote.

What else do you hear?

Mary returned his gaze soberly, and with an effort, she opened her ears.

The harness jingles when the horse moves its head. Its breath is loud.

Henry nodded.

There is a stream nearby running into the lake. There is wind. A bell, the school bell is ringing.

Henry nodded again, formed the word "thanks" with his mouth, and touched the reins lightly to the horse's back. Mary felt a sudden sting of tears in her eyes and turned her face away as the gig lurched forward.

"I'm sorry," she said aloud. "I'm sorry for you."

Her own voice was strange to her ears, rusty and cracked, like something that hadn't been used in a long time.

"I don't want to hear these things," she said. "Sometimes I can't bear to hear them. You know why. No one else here knows, but you do."

The road passed over a low-lying area crowded with last year's cattails and new green reeds shooting up and swaying in the breeze. As the gig rattled onward, the call of the red-winged blackbird came again, sudden and shrill, then again, answered on all sides. Mary shielded her eyes against the sun to watch as wave upon wave of blackbirds rose from the marsh, dipping, veering, singing out across the brilliant lake.

When they arrived at the house, Mary took the mail inside, and then went out to the carriage house with a memorandum book of blank pages. Henry had put a blanket over the horse and was shutting the door to its stall when Mary's shadow fell across his feet. He looked up in surprise.

May I speak to you about the war? Mary wrote, and held out the book to his gaze.

He beckoned her to follow, and led the way to a cozy room at the lake side of the carriage house. It was arranged as a sitting room for Henry, with a small stove, a table and some chairs, and shelves full of books. He indicated one chair and took the other so that they sat on opposite sides of the table. The room was very quiet, except for the occasional thump of the horse's heavy feet on the floor of the stall nearby. At the window, a creeping vine was opening its leaves against the glass, making a green shade, waving gently in the breeze.

Henry took a pen from the table, dipped it in the inkwell, and wrote in Mary's book. *They say you were a nurse.*

Mary nodded.

Then you know what the war was.

Mary nodded again.

Henry's pen scratched quietly. He frowned as he wrote. *No one here knows. They don't understand why I can't continue as before.*

For a moment, Mary bowed her head. She could barely remember what she had done before the war. She had loved her brother the way a rose loves the sun. Then the sun had gone, and everything was in shadow. She heard the scratching of Henry's pen as he wrote again.

I was frightened all the time. Sometimes I think the noise broke my heart.

Yes, Mary wrote. *Yes, I know.*

What did you want to ask me?

Where did you do your fighting?

Shiloh. Bull Run. Gettysburg.

Mary's heart tightened at the sight of *Gettysburg.* She began to write, *I had a brother. He*—but could write no further than that. Her hand clenched around the pen. She set it down across the paper.

Henry eased the paper out from under her hand and read it. He raised his eyes to hers. Mary heard the sounds of the carriage house beams settling and ticking, the tapping of the vine against the window, the twittering of swallows in the barn. She heard the sound of her own blood moving in her veins. Henry continued to look at her as though he could hear her heartbeat, too.

"This was a mistake, I'm sorry," Mary stammered. She picked up the pen to write, *I should not have brought up the war. I'm sorry.*

She pushed her chair back with a scrape and hurried out of the room, her footsteps echoing among the rafters.

Outside, she heard the crunch of gravel under her feet on the path to the kitchen door, heard the distant clattering of pots in the kitchen, heard the squeak of a window being slid open. At the kitchen step she stopped and looked back to see Henry standing in the carriage house doorway. When he caught her glance, he raised his hand in a wave, and the motion seemed to resonate against her where she stood.

Bells

WHAT DID THE members of the household think of this unspeaking girl? What did they make of the silent figure who moved among them like a sleepwalker, as removed from them all as the stuffed owl in its bell jar?

Dorsett told his wife he found Mary efficient, capable, and intelligent. Yet he had no proof of her intelligence, really, because she did not pester him with questions, did not seek to impress him with any knowledge that she had. She asked for nothing, complained of nothing, wanted nothing, and so when the naturalist looked up from his desk to see her sweeping the floor of the glasshouse, or putting away the microscope slides in their wooden cases, or placing photographs into the press to flatten them—all her movements attended by a grave solemnity, like a mournful bell tolling—he was moved to such pity that he would wrench off his glasses and say abruptly: Go out, Mary, take a walk, I don't need you just now. And silently, without protest or question, Mary would go.

In her turn, Diana Dorsett told her husband that she found Mary to have a remarkably delicate touch when the younger girl spent an hour some evenings brushing the woman's pale golden hair, so delicate that it was as though Mary might be touching her from some other world. Diana would study Mary's reflection in the mirror and tell stories about the wild land where she had grown up—the desperate winters, the luxuriant summer tumult of flowers, the flashing glories of the aurora borealis, the signal bells in Hudson Bay clanging with the tides—trying to draw a smile or a look of surprise from Mary, hoping to make that steady hairbrush pause or jerk just once.

Rose admitted to Diana that she had never found a more able helper, and it was certainly true that Irish girls were strong, and so far, knock wood, not a bit of trouble from her. Rose had only to think of the potatoes that needed peeling or the boots that needed cleaning, and Mary had bent her head to the task. On the instant that a bell rang over the kitchen door, Mary was gone to answer it without waiting to be told. But for kitchen company, Rose was a little disappointed in Mary. Mary would not speak, would not sit obligingly curious for stories and gossip, begging to be filled in on the history of the house. Nights, Rose would sit in her own room, knitting socks for missionaries, rocking in her rocking chair by the window, shaking her head. Once in a while she would pause in her rocking, as though a thought had come to her. But Mary was a thought that Rose could not comprehend. So the old woman would continue rocking, knitting, and shaking her head.

And Henry—Henry told no one what he thought of Mary. No one asked him what he thought of Mary.

But Mary began to speak to him.

She began one afternoon in the middle of May. Dorsett had asked for all the plants in the glasshouse to be moved outside, to be thoroughly watered and washed, and for the greenhouse itself to have a spring cleaning. Mary performed this task with Henry's aid. He carried the heavy potted plants out into the sunshine, placing them on flagstones in the courtyard or wooden benches along the outside wall of the greenhouse. Mary, wiping dust from the broad, glossy leaves of a rubber tree with a towel, said, "I've never washed a plant before."

She looked over at Henry. His back was to her as he put a small orange tree, bowed with fruit, on the ground. She resumed swabbing the thick leaves with the cloth. They squeaked faintly when she rubbed them between her fingers.

"I won't know what to do if Mr. Dorsett asks me to wash his stuffed birds."

She looked up, smiling a little. Henry turned and walked by her into the glasshouse again, noticing her smile and smiling in return as he passed.

From across the lawn came the light tinkle of a fairy bell. Nanuk was trying to stalk a robin, but the bell around his neck gave him away time and time again. The robin, tilting its head to listen, heard the bell each time Nanuk moved, and fluttered or hopped to a safe distance without ever having to look at the cat. The white cat continued to creep forward, body close to the grass, sure it would succeed. Mary breathed a sigh as she watched.

"You can't know how glad I am that you don't ask what makes me smile, Henry," she said. "Some of the matrons at the hospitals were full of suspicions, for they thought the Irish dishonest, and only let a girl crack a smile but they're thinking you've done a mischief. And the boys—all the time they were after asking what was I thinking of, but they only wanted me to say I was thinking of them. They were always after wanting a girl to be in love with them, for they knew they were soon dying. So I never told them what I truly thought.

"And the fellows at the Shinny, the saloon where I lived. They were the same, for although they weren't dying, they all felt they were tragic enough. The boyos at the saloon and the boyos in the hospital were like that Nanuk there, so sure I didn't know what they wanted, they must have thought me a rare fool. But they gave themselves away every time, talking, talking, talking. I thought I'd never hear an end to all their talking and wished I were deaf myself, and not a thing I could do to help them, for I can never love; nor not a one of them touched my heart, for I don't think I have one left in me.

"Och, Nanuk, y'stupid eejit," she said with a rush of anger. Mary stepped forward quickly and snapped the cloth at the cat, who bolted across the lawn, cross-eyed with alarm. Mary laughed as the tinkle of his bell faded away.

Henry's footsteps sounded behind her. Mary saw that he was struggling to get through the door without breaking off the flowers of a sprawling tropical plant. She reached out to help guide the fragile stems through the door, and one bell-shaped red flower fell from its stem as it brushed the frame. It dropped without a sound into the open neck of Henry's shirt as Mary helped him with his difficult load.

THUNDER

GRACE HARBOR WAS visited by a thunderstorm on a night late in May. Behind the large white house, where Dorsett had established a blind from which to photograph nesting bluebirds, the maples turned their leaves against the wind. The vine-covered gazebo shuddered under the pelting rain. In the vegetable garden, water ran between the furrows, seeking pea seeds that strained up through the mud. On the lake, the heaving water sprayed upward toward the clouds. The two small boats in the boat house bumped and knocked against their moorings. Racing sheets of rain swept down the windows of the house.

At the top of the stairs, lightning flashed through the oval window and brought the stuffed birds and mounted butterflies to momentary life, and sent sparks through the case filled with crystals. Gleams of lightning struck rainbows from the prisms of the dining room chandelier. Light darted over the stags' antlers and sent shadows like tree branches leaping across the downstairs hall.

The thunder knocked on the doors, making the finches hop nervously in their cage. It rattled the windows in their frames, as though trying to rouse the house from a deep sleep. Then it rolled over the rooftop and down the chimneys, waking Mary.

She lay in her bed in the dark, and in the flashes of lightning saw the shape of the books stacked beside her bed; they were books Henry had lent to her. Each thump and mutter of thunder told her that Henry was sleeping in his room above the carriage house, unaware of the storm, and she said out loud into the darkness, I must tell him about the thunder tomorrow, he will want to know.

A curious pattern had developed. When no one else was nearby, Mary spoke to Henry of her past life in Washington, where she had worked as a barmaid and a nurse; she spoke to him about her brother killed in the war and the father she had worked to send back to Ireland. These things she had to say out loud, but she did not want anyone to hear. She hoarded her voice like a miser with everyone else; with Henry, she spent it recklessly.

The things she heard, she told Henry of in notes and letters. In the kitchen, eating supper with Rose wheezing at the head of the table, Mary would write to him, *Mr. Dorsett was practicing bird calls in the darkroom today. He is very proud of his wood duck call.*

Mrs. Dorsett has hung in her window a string of shells from her cousins in Jamaica—they clink and tinkle when the breeze comes off the lake.

I think there are mice in the east wall of my room: there is a scratching sometimes in the night.

Rose has sniffles again. When she blows her nose, it honks.

Eating, Henry would watch her write, listening to the sounds she wrote. Sometimes he would write briefly, *Bacon frying is a good sound,* or *I think that red hen must be a noisy complainer—is she?*

Mary began to collect sounds for Henry. She gave him as many as she could.

In return, he let her talk and did not ask what she was saying. He gave her books. He showed her where the vegetable plants were sprouting in the garden, and once took her to see a nest of baby mice he had discovered in the barn. Sometimes, in an offhand way, he handed her a flower if he had been gardening, or a spray of mint, or a small crystal unearthed among the pea vines.

What do you hear? he would write to her when they crossed paths during the day.

And Mary would stop, and listen, and write, *Pot lids in the kitchen,* or *Mrs. Dorsett singing as she walks up the staircase,* or *Waves from the beach,* or *The coffee grinder has as many noises as beans; Rose is cranking it hard.*

So even as Mary lay awake listening to the thunder, she was telling Henry about the sound, the knock and tumble of it, the growl and mutter, and about how it had awoken her from a dreamless sleep.

Henry will want to know, she told her darkened room.

But as it happened, she had more than that to tell him in the morning. Dorsett called her into his study before breakfast, and there told her the errand he wanted her—and Henry—to do. They were to take Dorsett's collection of stuffed warblers to the Niagara Falls Seminary for Women, a small school run by a colleague of his. The birds were to be on loan for the day to illustrate the principles of differentiation among species, and although Dorsett had planned to take them himself, he had changed his mind: he wanted to spend the day in his blind, trying to photograph the bluebirds.

Therefore, Mary and Henry were to go, and while the school was using the warblers, they would be free to visit the falls. They were well worth visiting, Dorsett assured Mary with a smile, and only twenty miles away from Grace Harbor.

And so it was that by noon, having taken the spur line to the city of Niagara Falls and delivered the warblers in their cases to the seminary, Mary and Henry walked over a stone footbridge to Goat Island. Beneath the bridge, the turbulent flood of the Niagara River pouring out of Lake Erie foamed and bubbled around rocks, and whole tree trunks, dark and saturated with water, slammed against the banks before rushing on. Gulls wheeled screaming overhead.

Mary paused to watch the hypnotic rush of water. In the distance was another sound that she tipped her head to hear, an indistinct roar that seemed to come from all directions at once, almost as though it were the sound of the sunshine that flooded the area. Henry leaned on his elbows on the wall of the bridge.

Have you seen this waterfall before? Mary wrote. *Is it very big?*

Henry grinned as he read her question. *Haven't you ever heard of Niagara Falls?* Mary shook her head. *You'll see for yourself, then. What do you hear?*

I don't know. I don't know what it is.

He nodded his head toward the tree-covered island, and they walked on. Other tourists strolled by them, talking eagerly together, and vendors called out to hawk panoramic postcards, souvenir spoons, beaded Indian moccasins, peanuts and candy. Gulls were everywhere, arguing over bread scraps and heckling the tourists. And over all was the one great sound, growing louder and louder with each step Mary took along the path.

A feeling of apprehension began to take hold of her. She stopped where the path began to curve around a screen of trees. The noise was all around them.

Henry walked on ahead, not realizing she had stopped.

Mary's heart began to race. "What is that?" she whispered. "What is that noise?"

She moved forward slowly. As she rounded the corner, she saw Henry stopped in his tracks, and beyond him was the roaring cataract. Mary reeled backward slightly as she took it in, the impossible, giant cascade of water falling into the gorge far below. The cloud of mist rising from the torrent was like the steam from some titanic machine, and the flying gulls disappeared into it, tiny specks swallowed by the vapor.

"I didn't know," Mary stammered. She shielded her eyes against the sun with one hand, and with the other groped blindly for something to hold on to. She touched a railing and stood there, shaking her head.

A man climbing up the path gave her a look of concern. "Taken queer, are you? It takes many folks that way. Just catch your breath and you'll be on the gain in no time."

Mary kept shaking her head. "I didn't know it was so . . . big."

"That's the Canadian side of the falls, the Horseshoe," the man said with a sweep of his arm. "Hundred and sixty feet straight down. What you see there is the Great Lakes falling over a cliff. Say, is that your beau down there?"

Mary saw him pointing at Henry, and shook her head quickly. "Oh, no, no. He is my friend."

"Well, he looks like he might be taken a little queer, too; I'd watch out for him. Never even looked at me when I told him to mind the steps."

Mary didn't bother to explain, but hurried down the path to join Henry where he stood at the railing. He looked down at her with a smile, and Mary nodded. Then they turned to regard the falls, their faces bathed in mist.

The river above the precipice boiled and plunged headlong through the rapids, foaming blue-green. The ceaseless, relentless surge of the water was mesmerizing, and where it flowed over the edge into space it seemed almost to stand still. The sound was monstrous, and the wind the falls created buffeted Mary where she stood. She clutched the wet iron railing, staring and staring at the flow. Mist clung to her lashes, and she blinked it away.

Henry passed his notebook to her. *This goes on and on forever, no matter what men do in the world. It does not know mankind or our fights.*

Mary looked at the waterfall, looked at Henry, looked at the waterfall again. *Then I am glad for it being here,* she wrote.

There is a staircase to the bottom of the American Falls. I'd like to show you the cave there. Would you care to go down?

Almost in a daze, Mary nodded. She followed Henry along the edge of the rocky island that split the Niagara River in two and sent it cascading into the Niagara Gorge. The place was crowded with sightseers, and Mary was vaguely aware of a gabble of foreign languages, shrieks of excitement and cries of admiration, but it was all muted and dwarfed by the giant sound of the waterfall thundering into the chasm. Ahead was a painted wooden booth with a sign above, "Biddle Stairs: Cave of the Winds." Farther along was another plume of mist and spray rising from the second cataract, the American Falls. At the side of the booth, people were shrugging into full-length oilskin coats, laughing and joking and teasing one another in anticipation. A white-haired man was selling hot coffee from a pushcart to the wet and breathless tourists who pulled themselves up from down below. Shouts of "Oh, there's the top at last!" and "What a climb!" floated up the stairs with the mist.

"Like to brave the mighty waterfall in the Cave of the Winds, mister? Dollar per person," the man in the booth called out to Henry.

"He can't hear you," Mary said. She touched Henry's arm and pointed at the sign. Henry nodded. "We'll both go down," she added.

"Two dollars. Mind the wet. The stairs are plenty slippery, young lady. Step around to the side and find a coat that fits you," the man said. "Tell your friend to do the same."

As Mary moved to the side of the little building, she saw the Biddle Stairs, which were more a narrow wooden ladder than a staircase. The rickety structure snaked down the face of the cliff, secured with rusting iron bolts. Twenty yards away, the American Falls poured down the same cliff with a deafening roar. Mary peeked over the edge. Gusts of wind surged up into her face, but below she could see a narrow, glistening path hugging the rock, leading toward the cataract. She felt a touch on her shoulder, and turned to see Henry holding out a coat for her. She put it on, its damp weight pressing on her shoulders. Her fingers trembled as she fastened the buttons.

Now that Henry's notebook was stowed in a dry pocket, communication was impossible. They exchanged a look, and then began to descend. Each tread of the steep staircase was slick with water, and the railing dripped at the touch. Mary used one hand to keep her skirts out of the way as she climbed down. Nodding grasses poked out of the cliff face between the treads, and with each step Mary took, more and more of the American Falls came into view. The sound grew louder and more explosive the lower she went, and she felt the staircase shake with the force of the winds. Gusts of mist and spray blew against her. Her heart was pounding, but when Henry looked up at her, she found herself smiling in spite of her fear. Water dripped from his eyelashes and sparkled in the sunlight.

At the bottom, Henry reached up to help her down the last step. Their wet hands met for a moment, and then Mary hugged her oilskin coat tighter before they set off down the wet path. Puddles shone in the sun. Water dripped and trickled from a hundred fissures and cracks in the rock face. Huge boulders and bare broken tree trunks lay in gleaming, jumbled piles, and gulls circled above them, their cries drowned by the stupendous thunder of the falls.

At last, they reached the base of the waterfall, where the treacherous path led behind the cascade. The world was all water, pouring from above. Mary tipped her face up and was immediately drenched by splashes and mist. Then she drew a deep breath and stepped behind the face of the waterfall.

The path snaked around a boulder and suddenly opened into the Cave of the Winds. Mary and Henry stood amazed, bracing themselves against the strong swirling currents of air. The face of the cave was a solid wall of cascading blue-green water, and the western sun shining through it created a thousand circular rainbows that spangled and spun through the echoing cavern. Mary turned around and around, watching the rainbows, feeling herself swallowed by the terrible grandeur of the waterfall. The air was so thick with mist that she could hardly breathe. Never in her life had she imagined anything so overwhelming, so tremendous, as being inside a waterfall; never had she thought that nature could contain so much water, or that she could stand below it as it fell, a magnificent absolution. The very air and rocks vibrated with the power of the water, making the sound something that was inside Mary.

The thunder of the falls filled her, surrounded her, shook her and deafened her, and she knew she could hear no more than Henry could. She was as deaf as he was. She looked at him, dripping, his face shining with exhilaration as he gazed upon the sheet of water, and the giant sound pounded inside her until she found she was shouting as loud as she could.

"Henry! Henry!" she cried out, knowing that he could never hear her, unable to hear herself. "Henry!" And even as she yelled, she knew she wanted, more than anything, for him to hear the sound of her voice saying his name.

BOOK III

Is this then a touch? quivering me to a
new identity,
Flames and ether making a rush for my
veins

—Walt Whitman, "Song of Myself"

SLAP

DIANA DORSETT WAS a woman who loved texture, the touch of things, the nap and hand of fabrics, the roughness of bark, the silk of feathers and fur. She trailed through the house running her hands over the backs of the chairs, rubbing the velvet drapes at the windows, clicking her fingernails across the wires of the finches' cage, pressing her cheek against the cool windowpanes, stroking her cat.

Mary discovered that Diana didn't care how brightly the silver shone or how sharp the creases were ironed into the linen napkins. She did not entertain, did not insist on a lavish toilette. She went for long walks, read and wrote letters, directed the care of the flower gardens.

But she picked things up and set them down again in the wrong rooms, and sometimes, in the middle of an explanation about a chore that needed doing, Diana might pick up a fossilized clam shell or a boar's tusk and become lost in contemplating it with her fingers. Mary would have to wait, saying nothing, until the woman recalled what she was doing. Sometimes Diana would forget completely and walk away, leaving Mary to wonder what it was she was meant to do. At first Mary became anxious when this happened, sure that she would leave some vital task undone and be scolded for it.

And yet Mary found that her mistress never scolded or complained. Sometimes two or three days would go by when Mary was busy on Mr. Dorsett's behalf, and Mary only tidied Diana's room or changed the flowers, and if she did meet Diana on the stairs, the woman would smile and praise her for doing such good work for her husband.

"Mr. Dorsett speaks very highly of your skills," Diana said one morning. They were in the garden. Mary carried a basket of flowers while Diana bent to cut the blossoms she wanted from the peony bushes and early roses. "He says you have learned the workings of the darkroom wonderfully well."

"Thank you, ma'am."

Diana brushed the petals of a heavy, blushing

peony against her smiling lips, back and forth. Her gaze traveled across the lawn to the brush-covered blind by the bluebird house. Her smile widened.

"He's very optimistic about his bluebirds, isn't he? I hope he will make some fine photographs of them."

"He has two already, although he's not satisfied." Mary looked over at the blind. There was a wing-flash of blue, and then just in front of Mary's eyes flew a mosquito. She focused on it, and watched it sink down and settle on her hand. For a moment she only watched it, not noticing any sting. Then she slapped it. She knew she'd been bitten, because there was blood on her fingers, but she couldn't feel it. She rubbed the smear of blood away on the handle of the basket.

Diana waved off a mosquito, too, and bent again to the peonies. "Oh, dear, the return of the mosquitoes. In the north, the mosquitoes have such a short season that they all come out at once in great clouds. You can't go outside without being bitten within an inch of your life. Does it itch?" she added, tapping Mary's wrist with a pink flower.

"I suppose it does." Mary touched it absently.

"The Anishinabe have a story about First Mosquito. They say it was an old sorceress who hated all the human beings and persecuted them whenever she could, bringing evil thoughts to them and stinging them into argument. But brave Glooskap threw a pine tree at her, and it stuck in her side. It didn't kill her, but she retreated to the woods and shrank to a tiny size and sprouted wings. Of course she still hates human beings and stings them with that sharp pine tree whenever she can."

Mary scratched at her mosquito bite. It was beginning to itch. "Who are the Anishinabe, Mrs. Dorsett?"

"Oh, they are an Indian people. Their name simply means the human beings. I knew many of them in Canada. Anishinabe, Cree. And sometimes Inuit would come down the coast of Hudson Bay in their skin canoes to trade furs. The Inuit call themselves the human beings, too."

Mrs. Dorsett looked out at Lake Ontario as though watching a group of Inuit coasting toward her in their kayaks, their paddles flashing wet in the sunlight. Mary had a sudden vision of the woman as a young girl, alone among the fur traders, making friends with Indian children, separate but happy. Diana Dorsett had an air of being alone, had no children and saw few friends, and yet she never seemed to be lonely.

"We call ourselves Americans, Canadians, Irish . . . We don't call ourselves the human beings," Diana mused.

Mary heard the slap of waves on the beach below

the garden. "Perhaps because we know we are savages."

Mrs. Dorsett put her hand on Mary's, covering the mosquito bite. "Don't say that. You say that because you've seen savagery. But you know we can be noble and good and kind. Look at my husband. Can you say he is of a race of savage men?"

Just then, they saw Dorsett stride out of the greenhouse and make his way toward the blind, his coattails flapping behind him. He carried a glass plate holder, ready for the camera. He ducked inside, pulling the dark green curtain shut behind him. Rather than shoot the birds he loved, he would gladly spend hours hunched at his camera and ruin dozens of plates. Diana Dorsett's face had softened as she watched her husband.

"Can you say he is of a race of savage men?" she repeated softly.

"No. I can't."

"I knew the moment I saw Mr. Dorsett that he was the kindest, gentlest man on the earth," Diana said. "The October we met, he was negotiating the rapids on the Sachigo and lost his canoe, his shotgun, all his specimens. He walked north through the muskeg for two weeks until he reached Fort York. When he walked into my father's office, it was as though I'd been fast asleep and someone had patted my cheeks to waken me. I was so startled, so struck . . ." Her hand went to her cheek, and she caressed it as she spoke.

The woman's smile brought a sudden flare of heat to Mary's face. Her skin tingled hotly, and she looked away in confusion. The thought came to her that although Diana Dorsett was alone so often, she was never lonely, because she loved her husband so much, and he loved her greatly in return.

In the same instant, with the force of a slap, Mary knew that she herself was both alone and lonely. She had never had much to love, only her reckless, careless brother, and he was two years dead. Since then she had guarded herself too well against friendship, wrapping herself with invisible bandages while she bandaged wounds in the hospital.

Another mosquito landed on her wrist, and she slapped it hard. Tears stung her eyes and she cried out.

"Mary, what is it?"

"I've hurt myself," Mary gasped. "I've hurt myself."

She felt pins and needles prickling through her hand, as though it had fallen asleep and was now painfully, painfully waking up.

Brush

THE BLIND NEAR the bluebird house had been constructed behind a screen of mock orange bushes. The curtained back was unobstructed, easily reached from the greenhouse, and Jasper Dorsett had worn a path in the grass going to and fro with plates for the camera. As June progressed, the mock orange began to bloom, more and more white flowers bursting open every day. It provided excellent camouflage for the blind, and the bluebirds seemed oblivious to the man who watched them so eagerly from its cover.

And yet, the brush in front of the blind was beginning to grow too abundant. It had to be pruned, or else all the photographs would be crosshatched with leaves and flowers.

"Perhaps you and Henry can manage it together," Dorsett said to Mary, sorting through the papers on his desk one morning. "I don't want too much pruned, and we can't disturb the birds in the process."

Mary put away a box of microscope slides. "I can hardly look through the camera in the blind and call out to Henry which branches to cut. He won't hear me."

"No, no . . ." Dorsett pulled on his lower lip. "But I trust you to arrange things."

"Yes, Mr. Dorsett."

"Pity about Henry, though, isn't it?" Dorsett said abruptly. "Such a shame; he had such prospects. I expected him to make a fine scholar, but now he says he doesn't want—well, see what you can do about the brush, Mary."

Mary left the study in search of Henry. For some reason, she almost always knew where he was, although she never asked him what his chores for the day were. But she had discovered that when she needed to find him, she knew where he would be.

Now she found him in the garden, just where she expected to find him. He was hoeing potatoes, his Union Army forage cap shading his eyes from the morning sun. It was sometimes a shock to her to remember how he had been raised, the minister's cultured son. But Mary knew well how many dreams the war had broken. Mary dug her notebook from her apron pocket.

The brush in front of the blind needs trimming, she wrote.

Mr. Dorsett can't see his birds?

Mary smiled and shook her head. Henry pointed to the carriage house, and then held up one finger—wait a moment. Then he was gone, carrying the hoe back to the barn.

She waited for him among the potato hills. The ground he had been hoeing was dark with moist, turned earth. Mary bent down and took a handful of soil, crumbling it between her fingers. It was cool and damp, both soft and gritty at the same time. When she heard the door of the carriage house shut, she stood up, brushing the dirt from her hand and watching Henry return with a pair of long-handled pruning shears.

In step, they walked around the back of the house to the blind, Mary jotting a note in her book.

I'll have to look through the lens and let you know which branches to cut. There's an opening, perhaps I can point.

Henry nodded. There was a thumb-print smudge of garden earth on his cheekbone, and when Mary noticed it, she glanced down in confusion at the dirt on her hand, wondering if somehow she had touched Henry's face without realizing it. The next moment she flushed with embarrassment at such a wayward thought. She stepped quickly inside the blind and yanked the curtain shut behind her.

Inside, it was warm and dim. What light there was came filtered through the white canvas roof, and the shadows and silhouettes of the mock orange reached around the sides. Mary moved to the big box camera that peeked through the canvas at the bluebirds, pried off the lens cap, and peered through.

Several branches arched across her field of vision, and suddenly Henry stepped into view, frowning at the bushes. Mary could see quite clearly the smudge on his cheek, and again found herself brushing the dirt from her hand. Her fingertips felt dry and dusty against her apron.

It was obvious that there was no way to communicate with him through the blind. She tried to memorize the features of the offending branches and then went outside again.

I'll point them out from this side, Mary wrote. But even as she stared in among the flowering branches of the mock orange, she saw that the only way to be sure was if she squirmed into the shrubs and put her back against the canvas. In that way she would see the branches from the camera's position. She pointed at herself, and then into the mock orange.

Henry looked skeptically at the tangle of brush, looked at Mary, and grinned. He knew just what she intended, and made an elegant bow to usher her into the shrubbery.

"Well, now, Mr. Till, you needn't look so pleased with yourself."

Mary patted her hair. She knew the twigs would snag it, but she began to work her way in among the branches all the same. They snapped and rustled as she passed through, and the white blossoms brushed against her cheeks, smooth as kisses. Twigs and leaves snatched at her black hair, prickling her scalp. It was only a few steps to the canvas wall of the blind, and when she reached it, she stood close to where the camera's lens poked through, and turned to face out. Her view was now crisscrossed with a grid of branches that formed a cage in front of her.

Henry stood two arms' lengths away on the other side of the wall of brush. Mary put her hand on the first limb. Henry reached in with the pruning shears and clipped off the branch. It fell to the ground. She touched the next, and he cut that, and it fell to the ground. Mary watched him, watched how he opened up the way in front of her as he cut the next and the next and the next, until her path was clear. She nodded, and Henry reached his hand in to help her step back out into the sunshine again.

"Thank you," she whispered. She withdrew her hand from his and then hurried into the house.

"Missus has just rung for you," Rose announced as Mary entered the kitchen.

"Yes, I'll just wash my hands." Mary went to the sink and worked the pump handle until a stream of water gushed out. She put her hands in the stream and washed the garden soil away. The water was cold, and she splashed some onto her cheeks. She felt flushed. Through the window over the sink she could see the blind where Henry was dragging the brush away.

When Mary entered Mrs. Dorsett's room a few moments later, the woman was sitting at her dressing table. Diana met her eyes in the mirror and turned around in surprise.

"Why, Mary, what have you been doing?"

"Ma'am?" Mary put her hands to her hot cheeks.

Laughing, Diana rose and walked toward her. "You look as though you've been playing in the woods." She reached out and pulled a leaf from Mary's hair.

Mary blushed even deeper and her hands now

went to her hair. "I beg your pardon, ma'am. I didn't know I was such a sight."

"Well, I was going to ask you to brush my hair, but I think our positions must be reversed this morning," Mrs. Dorsett said with another laugh. "Come. Sit here."

Ignoring Mary's protests, Diana led her to the dressing table and pushed her gently down onto the seat. The woman picked up her hairbrush and drew the pins that held Mary's long hair up.

"Now, sit still like a good girl," Diana said firmly.

Mary sat as rigid as a statue as her mistress began to brush her hair. Nobody had brushed Mary's hair since she was a very small girl and her mother died, and the touch of another hand on her head was a shock. And for it to be her employer was even more shocking. Appalled, she watched herself in the mirror, watched Diana's head bent over hers and the strong, steady strokes of the brush.

"I used to do this with my Cree playmates when I was a little girl," Diana reminisced. "We brushed one another's hair for hours on end. Didn't you?"

"No, ma'am," Mary whispered. "I never did."

In spite of herself, Mary closed her eyes and tipped her head back. These people refused to treat her as a servant. They insisted on being kind. They insisted on making life good. The luxury of another person caring for her filled Mary with peace.

"Poor thing. Imagine never having someone brush your hair for you," Diana murmured. "If I had ever had a little girl, I know I would have done nothing but brush her hair."

The pull of the brush through Mary's hair set her scalp tingling, just as the snagging twigs and leaves had done. She closed her eyes and saw herself in among the mock orange again, watching the spiky branches fall away as Henry cut one by one through the bars that surrounded her, and let her out.

Stroke

IN THE GREEN-GABLED boat house were a small sailboat and a dinghy, which was painted red with blue seats. They were seldom used. Dorsett had once delighted in rowing along the edges of the lake on still mornings, observing the ducks and shorebirds. But ever since he became interested in photography, the boats had rested idly in their berths.

In July, however, as the days turned sultry, Henry asked permission to take the dinghy out from time to time, and one evening after dinner, as Mary sat at her open window writing a letter, she saw the little red boat approaching through the sunset from some distance across the lake.

She paused in her writing. It was the first letter she had written since her arrival, and she was finding it difficult to form her words. *Dear Mr. Walt,* she had written, *I have been here for three months now*, and had gone no further. The pen lay still in her hand, the ink drying in the nib.

The rowboat came slowly nearer to shore, and Mary could make out Henry bent to the oars. He rowed steadily, each stroke followed by a pause as the boat glided forward. Stroke, glide—Mary closed her fists as though around the handles of the oars and felt the resistance and give of the water, the smooth coast across the surface. The oars dipped and lifted, and the boat's wake veed out behind the stern, the water catching the red evening light and making an arrow of the boat, headed for the house.

Mary bent to her letter, dipped her pen. *The people here are so kind to me. You would like them, I am sure. They hardly treat me as a servant at all, and they do not care that I'm Irish, as many do.* The pen whispered in the quiet room. She could feel the texture of the paper communicated through the scratching nib. With an occasional glance through the window, she matched the strokes of her pen with the strokes of the oars as Henry rowed nearer to her. *I have been reading many books and discussing them with my new friend. I am learning photography. My work does not seem hard to me, I have had much harder. The hospitals are very far away now. Sometimes I am happy. I hope you are well.*

As she watched, Henry maneuvered the boat into the boat house and disappeared from her view. Sleepy birds called from among the darkened trees outside.

Thank you for finding me this position. I am very grateful.

I remain your friend, Mary Mehan.

She carefully addressed the envelope to Walt Whitman in Brooklyn, cleaned the pen, and corked the ink. Then she sat, watching out the window into the twilight for Henry to emerge from the boat house. Knowing where he was was important to her. He was her ally. He knew her. She knew him.

From below, a door shut softly.

"Jasper?" Diana Dorsett's voice came up from the lawn. "Darling, it's getting late."

Mary leaned out. Diana, a white, luminous figure against the grass, moved toward the bluebird blind. Mary watched as Diana put her hand to the curtain and then stepped inside. A moment passed. Mary heard the birds call again, heard the distant whisper of waves. Then Diana flung back the curtain, crying out.

"Mary! Help me!"

Mary's chair crashed backward as she jumped up and ran out into the attic passageway. Rose stepped out of her own room, knitting in hand. "Whatever is it?"

"I don't know," Mary answered on the run.

She hurried down two flights of stairs as fast as she could, and out of the house to the back lawn. As she began running toward the blind, she saw Henry starting up from the boat house, and when he saw her, he began to run, too.

"Mrs. Dorsett!"

Mary burst into the blind. It was dark inside, but she could make out Diana's white form huddled on the grass beside a darker shape.

"Mr. Dorsett is insensible," the woman gasped. "I can't rouse him. Darling, my darling, speak to me!"

Mary knelt beside Dorsett. She heard his labored breathing and saw a glint from his open eyes.

"Is it some kind of fit?" she whispered, taking the man's hand. It was icy.

Henry entered the dark tent, and Diana rose to grab his arm. "Henry—oh, you can't hear me! Mary, what do we do?"

In the darkness it was impossible to communicate with Henry except by touch. Diana pulled him toward her husband, and he bent to lift the man by the shoulders. Mary took Dorsett's feet, and they carried him as fast as they could out of the blind and into the house as Rose hurried to meet them with a lamp.

"Dear Lord, what is it?" the cook asked. In the light of the lamp, they could all see Dorsett staring up at them without a trace of recognition. Diana led the way into the parlor, and Henry and Mary laid him on a divan. Diana knelt at his side, stroking his hand and crying.

Henry touched Mary's shoulder, and when she looked at him, he formed the word *doctor*, and left the room. A few minutes later, as the three women hovered in silence over the stricken man, they heard the bay's hooves scattering gravel on the drive.

"Mary, what has happened? You must know." Diana looked up at Mary from the floor where she knelt. "Why can't he speak? Does he hear me?"

"This is not the nursing I know," Mary said. "But we must keep him warm while we wait for Henry to return with the doctor. Rose, some brandy, a hot water bottle . . ."

Mary stood looking down at Dorsett, watching his chest rise and fall as he breathed, avoiding the open eyes that did not see her. Then she hurried from the room in search of a blanket as Rose bustled away toward the kitchen, sobbing.

Dead, glassy bird eyes stared at her as she climbed the stairs. She had been almost happy, almost at peace, but now the weight of sickness and dying came flooding into her again, blinding and deafening, stealing the touch of the banister away from her fingers. She dragged a blanket from a linen cupboard and returned to the parlor, her senses numb.

Without speaking, she laid the blanket across Dorsett. Diana had loosened the black silk tie from around his throat and dragged a footstool to his side. She sat there now, stroking his cheek. Mary looked down at the woman's white fingers moving across Dorsett's tanned face. She had seen many women do as much with their hurt and dying boys and husbands. She had not expected to see it again. She was appalled and resentful to be seeing it again.

She stood in the shadows outside the circle of lamplight. When Rose returned with the hot-water bottle, Mary placed it on Dorsett's chest under the blanket. For a few agonizing minutes, they tried to force a drop or two of brandy between his lips, but as it spilled out from the corners of his mouth, Diana began to weep so hard that Mary made her drink the liquor instead. Then they kept watch and waited for the doctor.

In the hour that they waited, Dorsett seemed to diminish before them, growing frail and delicate. His cheeks appeared sunken, making his nose more sharp and beaklike than ever, his eyes as glazed and unseeing as the glass eyes of the birds that filled the room.

Mary found it impossible to stay in the parlor, listening to Rose sniffling into her handkerchief and watching Diana stare at her husband. She went to the front door with another lamp to watch for the doctor's shay, and when he finally arrived, she led the way to the parlor.

"What happened, can you tell me?" Dr. Howard asked as he removed his coat.

"I found him this way," Diana quavered. "What is wrong with him?"

The doctor felt Dorsett's pulse, peered into his eyes. "I suspect a cerebral accident, a stroke to the brain."

Rose wailed out loud. Diana pressed her hands together. "Will he recover?"

Dr. Howard, a dark, whiskery man who was the image of General Grant, led Diana to a chair and waited until she sat. "My dear Mrs. Dorsett, I cannot say for certain. He may. But he may have some impairment of speech, or be unable to move. We must wait and see."

He turned abruptly and looked at Mary. "You are the girl with some nursing, is that right?"

"Yes, doctor."

"Very good. We must get him into his bed, keep

him warm. By morning he may be able to take some food. If he can, he must have broth, porridge, some spirits diluted with water if he can take it."

When Rose began to wail even louder, Dr. Howard glared her way. "And he must be kept as quiet as possible. No hysterics."

Henry entered the room behind Mary. The doctor beckoned him forward, and between the two of them, they lifted Dorsett to carry him upstairs. As they did, the blanket slipped off and fell in a heap on the carpet. Before Mary could move to retrieve it, Diana had bent to pick it up and then stood holding it in her arms as the doctor and Henry carried Dorsett from the parlor. Mary followed them, but at the door she turned to look back. Diana stood like a white statue in the middle of the room, staring down at the blanket and stroking it with one hand as though it were her husband's face.

GRAVITY

JASPER DORSETT'S STROKE brought a new routine to the household. For the first four days he did not regain his senses, but lay in his bed staring sightlessly at the ceiling. Mary and Diana took turns feeding him. Some of the time he swallowed the soup or porridge they spooned into his mouth. Often he did not. They tried to keep him clean, but it was difficult and wearying, and at least once every day Henry helped Mary move Dorsett so that she could change the sheets. The laundry boiler was in constant use, and the clothesline was always filled with white linens drying in the steamy heat.

Mary carried the heavy laundry basket outside and felt the sun press down on her. She pinned the wet, burdensome sheets on the line, where they hung limp and wrinkled from the mangle. She ironed them when they were dry, picking up one hot iron and letting it thump down onto the board, then putting it back on the stove and hefting another iron. The weight of the irons and the heavy drape of the sheets seemed to pull her down as though they had acquired some new gravity. Her arms were leaden. Her walk had slowed as though she lifted each foot from thick mud.

And her head often felt too heavy to lift. On the morning four days after Dorsett's stroke, she paused outside his bedroom door and heard Diana inside, talking to her husband in a broken voice. Mary turned away. She felt she must keep her mind from bending toward Diana's grief and Dorsett's helplessness. She felt she might sink under their weight. All around her, the household was crushed by calamity, and she was horrified by the gravity of it. She was horrified that it would crush her, too. She could not bear it.

The door opened and Diana stepped out, wiping her eyes. She looked exhausted. "Mary, will you and Henry please change the linens on Mr. Dorsett's bed? I must take a nap; I've been up all night."

"Yes, ma'am." Mary turned to go back downstairs in search of Henry. She found him in the kitchen and beckoned him to follow her. She did not bother to explain. She had not written a note to him since the night Dorsett was stricken.

With Henry following her, Mary pulled herself up the stairs. In silence, they entered Dorsett's bedroom. Mary tried not to look at the man as she and Henry lifted him to one side of the wide bed. She did not want to see how diminished he was. She did not want to see him silent and unhearing, unresponsive to the touch of their hands.

Mary stripped the sheets from the free side, and then they moved Dorsett again so she could strip the other side. Then, laboriously shifting him from one side to the other again, they put clean linens on the bed and pulled the light coverlet over him. Dorsett's eyes were open all the time, but he did not see them.

Then, still in heavy silence, they gathered the soiled sheets and left the room. As Mary carried the linens to the washtub, she realized Henry was still following her, but she felt the claims of the people around her were so heavy that she could not turn around to look at him.

He thrust a notebook at her. She read the message without touching the book, barely turning her head.

You don't talk to me anymore.

She had no answer for him. She wiped a strand

of hair from her damp forehead. Henry wrote in the book again, and again thrust it in front of her.

I know *how often you spoke to me!*

With a weary shrug, Mary began her struggle with the laundry, but Henry took her arm and pulled her around.

Don't, he wrote. *Please don't go away.*

"I'm not," she said dully.

Yes you are. You should talk. You should talk to Dorsett.

He can't hear me.

Neither can I. That did not stop you before.

Mary felt a hot rush of anger and grief.

Patiently, insistently, Henry wrote again in his notebook. *If you won't talk to me, talk to Dorsett. Talk to Mrs. Dorsett. She's so frightened and lonely.*

Mary's head pounded.

Please talk to them.

"No, you talk to them!" Mary cried out. "You haven't lost your voice as well as your hearing! You talk to them!" She grabbed the notebook from him and wrote, *You could talk if you wanted to. Nothing prevents you. You could talk to* me.

A flush swept over Henry's face as he read. He raised his eyes to meet hers.

Ashamed and angry, Mary turned and fled. She burst through the laundry room door and went outside, ducking under the clothesline and running down toward the water.

The lake was as smooth and glassy as ice. As she ran toward it, she felt the humid breath of the grass under her feet and heard the dull, tired wash of the swell against the shore. At the water's edge she stopped, panting. Already she was hot and sweating from the short run in the heat. Her hair hung heavily against her neck. Her clothes pressed against her, clinging and damp, like the touch of fevered hands asking her: Mary, make me feel better, please help me, I need water, nurse, please, nurse . . .

Without thinking, she sat and unlaced her shoes and peeled off her stockings. Then she lifted the hem of her dress and waded into the water. The touch of it on her skin made her gasp. She pushed deeper, and pushed deeper again, dropping her heavy dress as she went. The skirt billowed out around her on the water. She waded farther, stretching her arms out to the coolness. Bit by bit, it began to ease the anger, and the hurt, and the weary lonesomeness that had been so heavy for so long. For a moment she stood, breathing deeply, and the pain began to ebb, like water poured from a glass.

She turned and looked back at the house. The

pains and fears of the people in it were loud in her ears, the clasp of their hands on hers was strong. Each of them was suffering, each of them wanted her to help them, broken birds brought in by the cat.

But she was one of them, too. She was calling to them, and she was clinging to their hands, and she suffered and wanted them to help her. They had made themselves her family. She owed them everything.

"I can bear it," she whispered, sinking back into the deeper water.

She floated. Her gravity left her.

BOOK IV

Far, far in the forest, or sauntering later
in summer, before I think where I go,
Solitary, smelling the earthy smell,
stopping now and then in the silence

—Walt Whitman, "These I Singing in Spring"

Rose

HE WAS GETTING better. There was no doubt of it, each day Dorsett improved a little bit. Diana and Mary eagerly measured his progress: yesterday the light of consciousness in his face, today following them with his eyes.

"Did you see that, Mary?"

"Yes, Mrs. Dorsett, I did."

"Jasper, my darling, do you hear me?"

Mary poured warm water into a basin and soaked a towel in it. "Perhaps he hears you, but can't tell you so yet," she offered as she brought the basin to the bed.

"Yes, you must be right. Yes."

And Mrs. Dorsett picked up her book again and

continued to read aloud in her low, quiet voice. She was reading Darwin to her husband. She sat with her back very straight, her book tipped toward the light from the blue-curtained window. Mary washed Dorsett's hands and face, and the soapy steam from the washbasin rose into her own face as she listened to Diana read.

" 'The sense of smell is of the highest importance to the greater number of mammals—to some, as the ruminants, in warning them of danger; to others, as the Carnivora, in finding their prey; to others, again, as the wild boar, for both purposes combined.' "

Diana's voice murmured in the peaceful room. Mary dipped the towel in the basin again and ran it lightly down the bridge of Jasper Dorsett's nose while she met his eyes. She thought perhaps he was attempting to smile. "I know you can hear her," she whispered, bending near his ear.

" 'In those animals which have this sense highly developed, such as dogs and horses, the recollection of persons and of places is strongly associated with their odour; and we can thus perhaps understand how it is, as Dr. Maudsley has truly remarked, that the sense of smell in man "is singularly effective in recalling vividly the ideas and images of forgotten scenes and places." ' "

Mary thought suddenly of the white roses that

grew up the hot south wall of the stable, and how the day before she'd paused to watch the bees working furiously among them, their legs covered with golden dust. She had lingered there, observing them, feeling the heat of the sun reflected from the building, and Henry had walked toward her and she had smiled.

She looked down at her hands in the water, at the round cake of soap floating like a white rose in the basin, and smiled again. Without interrupting Diana's reading, Mary placed the basin on the tray along with Mrs. Dorsett's breakfast and Mr. Dorsett's bowl of porridge. Diana's voice followed her as she left the room.

On the upstairs landing, Mary paused at the oval window that overlooked the lake. From there, she could just make out the corner of the stable and the white blur that was the spray of roses. She had gone to the stable to tell Henry—tell him something, she wasn't sure what at the time. She had just come from Dorsett's office, where she had read his mail and ordered it in degrees of importance. She had *known* the degree of importance of each letter, and she was amazed and delighted, and she wanted to tell Henry something about that. He was always the one she thought of first now, when there was something she wanted to say—but the white roses had caught her attention, and when she saw him, she completely forgot her errand, and could only smile.

Mary shifted the heavy tray in her hands and made her way down the stairs. In the kitchen, Rose was shaking her head over the table and chopping vegetables. "I don't know, I just don't."

"What is it, Rose?" Mary drew off water from the boiler, and began to wash the breakfast dishes.

"I do think I should see the doctor," the cook muttered. "But such an expense."

"You know Mrs. Dorsett will pay for the doctor," Mary said. "What is it this time?"

"Whatever is it all the time? My nose! So stuffed I can't smell a thing, and here I am a cook and I don't know what to do about it. I can't tell what I'm cooking."

"Mrs. Dorsett hasn't complained," Mary said.

"Of course she wouldn't, the lamb. She never complains about a thing, but that doesn't mean my cooking is what it should be." Rose let out a prodigious sigh, and then snuffled loudly. "See? Onions I'm cutting, and I can't smell a bit of it. If they weren't making my eyes water and I couldn't see them, how would I know what I'm chopping up?"

Mary dipped a porcelain teacup into hot water to rinse it, and toweled it dry. "I promise you, those are onions, Rose. I can smell them from here, even if you can't."

As she heard her own words, Mary froze with the teacup in midair. Blocking out the smells of chloroform and dying flesh and sickness in the army hospitals had been difficult, but she had accomplished it so well that she had ceased to notice any odors or perfumes at all. Her sense of smell had fallen asleep with all her other senses. But now she smelled onions from across the room.

Carefully, she placed the teacup on the counter and went to the table where Rose was working. As the cook looked on in surprise, Mary bent low over the chopped onions and inhaled deeply.

"What are you doing with your face in that mess, Mary? For pity's sake!"

The garden door opened, and Henry walked in, wiping his feet on the mat. He looked at Mary with some surprise.

Stinging tears welled up in her eyes. She was smelling, for the first time in a year. "I'm smelling the onions."

"You're sure they've got a smell?" Rose asked dryly. "Don't you think you ought to get a little bit closer?"

Mary laughed and wiped the tears from her cheeks. She met Henry's puzzled gaze. "I'm quite sure they've got a smell. And they smell as sweet as roses to me."

Smoke

IN THE LATE, hot afternoon, the doctor called again to check on Dorsett. He made his examination while Mrs. Dorsett and Mary waited at the opposite end of the room, and from time to time sent a quick look their way from under his heavy eyebrows.

"He is improving, wouldn't you say, doctor?" Mrs. Dorsett asked. Her face was pale and she was obviously tired. Her hands washed themselves together at her waist.

The doctor scowled. "I would say that his ability to focus his eyes on us is a hopeful sign. I would say that."

"What can we do?"

"Continue doing as you are doing, madam." He tucked his instruments back into his bag, and then with a graceless, jerking movement he strode to Mrs. Dorsett and took her hands. "You must not make yourself ill with worry. You must have strength and you must have courage."

Mrs. Dorsett nodded quickly, wanting to believe him. "Yes, doctor. I will."

Mary moved toward the door and held it for him, and Dr. Howard followed her out of the room.

"See to it Mrs. Dorsett gets some rest, too," the doctor ordered as they went down the stairs. "She's going to fret herself into a nervous condition."

"Yes, doctor."

Rose joined them at the bottom of the stairs, anxious for news. "He's on the mend now, isn't he?"

"Time will tell. Time and good nursing." The doctor paused at the front door and gave Mary a sharp look. "You're a very good nurse."

"Thank you, doctor."

"She's a good girl, is our Mary," Rose put in.

Dr. Howard regarded them both. "I can use a nurse. Plan to stay on here indefinitely, Mary, or go on to other things?"

Mary held the door. "I have no plans."

"You needn't stay a domestic, you know. An intelligent young woman like you. You've given no thought to your future?"

Mary looked down. "No, sir. I never think of the future. Never."

"Never?"

"When I was in the hospitals, sir, the boys liked to tell me about their plans and dreams for the future. I believe now it's best not to set any store by such plans. I believe that."

The doctor grunted. "All girls have their plans. It's only natural."

Mary held the door open, her chin set stubbornly. "I don't suppose I'm much like other girls, sir. Good evening, sir."

Dr. Howard looked as though he'd like to say something sharp in reply. But he only gazed about himself for a moment, and the stuffed birds returned his gaze without comment. At last, he shot his cuffs, straightened his necktie, and took himself off.

"A bit pert to him, weren't you, Mary?" Rose asked. "And what's all that gloom about, not thinking of the future? Some of your funny Irish fancies, is it?"

Mary shut the door. "Rose, I don't, that's all."

There was nothing more to say about it. Mary returned to the sickroom. The evening wore on and she made herself useful to Mrs. Dorsett in small ways. The room had grown stifling, so she opened every window wide to catch the breeze. The shaded lamp began to gutter, so Mary turned it down. A thin coil of smoke rolled upward against the window, where the sun was going down hot and orange over the lake. Behind the barn, a pile of brush that Henry had burned smoldered in the golden haze.

Mary stood by the window. The evening was still and hot, Lake Ontario was a pool of honey, and the smell of the smoke from the brush pile mingled with the green perfume of cut grass and the sourish tang of the tonic Dr. Howard had left for Dorsett. Mary heard a sizzle as the sun dipped into the lake, and she knew it was only the sound of a moth singed against the lamp.

But she also knew that from that time forward, the odor of smoke would always bring that hot evening and that scene to her mind, so she studied it. She studied the shapes of the trees growing dark and indistinct on the lawn. She studied the heat of the room pressing against her face. She studied the fine cracks in the paint on the window sash. She studied the quiet breathing of the sick man on the bed behind her. She studied it all so that she would always have a picture of complete quiet and peacefulness to hold against whatever pains might lie ahead. She studied it as an investment against a future she would not let herself imagine. She had not been completely truthful when she told Dr. Howard she did not let herself imagine the future: she only did not allow herself to imagine or expect that the future would be pleasant and joyful.

The horizon clung to its color while Mary stood at the window, and then released it to the dark. She turned back to the room. By the bed, Mrs. Dorsett had fallen asleep in her chair. Mary tiptoed across the room and went out, closing the door softly behind her, and then took herself upstairs to her own bedroom.

She awoke at the touch of Mrs. Dorsett's hand on her shoulder. The twilight breeze had long stopped, and the house was hotter than ever. Outside it was full night.

Mrs. Dorsett stood in a pool of light from her lamp. "I'm sorry, Mary. I'm sure Mr. Dorsett is very uncomfortable," she murmured. "We must get him somewhere cooler."

"The side porch?" Mary asked. There was a second-floor sleeping porch at the side of the house.

"It's very late, but I'm afraid you must wake Henry. I—" Mrs. Dorsett paused, as if suddenly realizing the impropriety of sending a young woman to a young man's bedroom.

"It's not a bother to me, missus," Mary said. "I've seen many young men in their beds." When Mrs. Dorsett stared, Mary added, "In the hospital, Mrs. Dorsett."

"Oh. Of course."

Mary drew a shawl around her shoulders and scratched a match into flame to light a candle. She followed Mrs. Dorsett down the attic stairs, and they parted on the second-floor landing. "Hurry, please," Mrs. Dorsett said as she turned to go into the sickroom. Her skirts rustled in the silent hallway.

Mary padded quickly down the stairs. The house seemed to pulse with heat, and even her candle added to it. She could feel the flame like a small sun against her cheek. Her shadow slipped along behind her within her small circle of light. Gleams from mirrors and glass eyes flowed past her. She lifted the latch on the back door.

The whir of tree frogs and insects greeted her, rising and falling all around her. Beyond the flame of her candle, fireflies winked on and off, signaling their desires to one another, hovering about one another in the moist, fragrant darkness. Within moments, lovesick moths began to circle her light. Farther away, the unseen lake licked the shore, small waves kissing the shoulder of the lawn. The air was heavy and warm, with stray scents of grass and roses and hot stones, and beneath all the other scents was the scent of the brush pile smoke. It drifted across the lawn from behind the stable, prickling Mary's nose.

Like a sleepwalker, Mary stepped into the night, and at the touch of gravel against her bare feet, she took to the grass. She moved across it toward the stable, her light glimmering like a firefly in the darkness.

When she reached the carriage house door, she leaned her weight against it. It swung open heavily, and when she raised her candle high, the light flowed up the stairs to the apartment where Henry slept. In the dancing candlelight, the door at the top of the stairs flickered like a flame. In the nearby stall, the horse shifted on its hooves, and Mary felt the prickle of bits of straw under her own feet. From behind her came the musical trill of the frogs.

Henry could not hear the frogs. He could not hear her. Mary climbed the stairs and pushed the door open and stepped into his room. He was asleep in his bed, by an open window screened with muslin. Slowly, Mary crossed to the bed and stood looking down at him. Her candle cast the shadow of his eyelashes on his cheeks. She held it closer, knowing she must wake him, but wanting, just for a moment, only to look at him. The smoke from her candle drifted up into her face like incense, and the odor of smoke clung to Henry as though he himself had been on fire. Mary leaned closer, closing her eyes and inhaling the scent of the smoke.

And then, as she leaned toward Henry, she tipped the candle and a stream of wax pattered onto the pillow by his head. Mary drew in her breath sharply, and at that moment, Henry opened his eyes.

If he was surprised to find her at his bedside, he did not show it. He looked up at her and whispered, "Mary."

Mary felt a great gathering up of her heart. "Henry, you spoke to me."

For a moment, they only looked at each other. The candle smoke wavered between them, and then there was a faint, sleepy bird call from far off and Mary remembered Jasper Dorsett.

She stood back and pointed toward the house. "Mr. Dorsett," she said, fanning herself to mime heat, and Henry, watching her, nodded.

He made as if to get out of bed, and Mary was about to turn away when he noticed the wax on his pillow, and Mary knew that he saw it and knew that he understood she had been watching him sleep. He looked at her again with a level gaze.

"I'll–I'll meet you at the house," Mary stammered. She hurried down the stairs and out of the carriage house so quickly that when she stepped outside her candle was snuffed by the wind of her motion. Mary was left with the smell of smoke spiraling upward into the dark sky.

Bouquet

THE CELLAR OF the Dorsett house was as full of wonderful samples and specimens as the upper floors, but these were of a different kind. The root cellar was a museum of jars, the product of Rose's weeks of summer and autumn labor from the previous year. Row upon row of jewel-colored jars lined the shelves: jars golden with brandied peaches or pickled corn, garnet with strawberry preserves, emerald with beans.

And in the wine cellar stood tall racks of bottles, each one labeled as meticulously as the naturalist's precious wrens and pipits. Since first arriving at the house, Mary had made many trips into the wine cellar to retrieve the bottles Mr. Dorsett requested.

Now, following Dr. Howard's instruction, Mary fetched bottles of port wine to bolster Dorsett's strength. Until his stroke, he had always uncorked his wine himself. It was a task that gave him pleasure, he claimed, and his wife teased that he delighted in hearing the pop of the cork. But since he had become incapacitated, Mary had learned to draw the corks herself.

So it was that the morning after her midnight visit to Henry's bedside, she had to go down to the cellar for a new bottle of wine. She held her lamp high as she descended the cellar stairs, and her hand brushing along the banister raised a current of cool air. She stopped and smelled the white-washed wall. Then she raised the hand that had touched the banister and smelled it. She held the lamp low before her and smelled the hot oily smoke rising from the chimney. Mary smelled her way all the way down the stairs, thorough as a hound, remembering aromas and odors from forgotten places. Mustiness, dampness, stone, distant mice, old lumber.

Slowly, she followed her nose into the wine cellar, sniffing the labels on the racks even as she read them. The light of the lamp glided across the round green glass of the bottles and threw up long shadows. She smelled mold and cobwebs and lead paint. She wanted to smell everything.

Once Mary found the correct bottle she put the corkscrew to work, and then raised the cork to her nose as she had seen Dorsett do. The bouquet of the wine was sharp and rich. Closing her eyes, she wafted the bottle in front of her, letting the aroma rise into her face.

And all in a moment she was back in the Shinny, the beery saloon she had called home for two years. On the turn of the New Year of 1864, Dooley the barkeeper had gathered his wife and Mary in the kitchen and shared a bottle of wine with them. "To the restoration of the Union," he toasted. "And God bless us all."

"And may our dear girl soon find a fine young fellow to carry her away from all this strife," added Mrs. Dooley, giving Mary a squeeze.

"Go on with you now," Mary whispered into the cool musty air of the Dorsett cellar, and the bouquet of the sweet wine moved at her breath.

She opened her eyes, and taking the lamp in one hand and the wine bottle in the other, she made her way back up the stairs to the kitchen. Rose had sliced up and salted a bushel of cucumbers and set them to drain before pickling. The cook wiped her hands on an apron and took the wine from Mary.

"I'll take it up," Rose said. "I'm going up in a moment."

"That's fine, then," Mary replied.

At the table, Henry was eating a piece of cherry pie and reading the newspaper. Mary felt a flutter of embarrassment at seeing him, but without looking up, he tapped the open notebook that lay beside the newspaper. Reluctantly, Mary leaned over the table to read it. She was not sure what to expect.

Take a row in the boat with me later?

Mary paused to consider. On their ride to town for the daily shopping, neither of them had alluded to the previous night. She herself did not know how to allude to it, did not know what she thought about it. Henry glanced up at her, waiting for her reply. For once, Mary felt that his silence was unbearable. She could not guess what he was thinking, what he thought of her watching him sleep.

Take a row in the boat with me later? she read again.

If Mrs. Dorsett says I may, she wrote while Rose bustled about with tray and wineglass.

He read her note and nodded, and turned back to the newspaper. Mary found she was staring at his hair, wondering what it smelled like, picturing herself at his bedside with the candle in one hand and putting her face against his neck to smell the smoke in his hair. Her head swam.

"I may not be able to go," she stammered, and hurried out into the sunshine.

"Go where?" she heard Rose ask as the door swung shut behind her.

A fine young fellow to carry her away from all this strife, Mrs. Dooley had wished.

"It can never be," Mary said.

She paced across the lawn to the gazebo, where honeysuckle made a scarlet tangle among the railings. Two swallows flitted out of the leaves as she approached, and she flung herself onto the seat. Her heartbeat sounded *Henry, Henry, Henry* against her ears.

She could not say it to herself, she could not open the way to the thoughts that darted about her like the swallows that darted in and out of the gazebo. Mary closed her eyes tight, stopped her ears, pretended not to notice the touch of leafy tendrils whispering against her neck. But all around her was the heady, sweet perfume of the honeysuckle, and she could not shut it out without ceasing to breathe.

"Mary! Mary! Come quickly!" Mrs. Dorsett's voice came to her from an upstairs window.

Startled, Mary ran out of the gazebo and looked up, shielding her eyes from the sun. Diana Dorsett leaned from the sickroom window, her dress a brilliant white against the blue curtains. She was beaming, as joyful as a bride.

"He spoke to me! He knows me!" she sang out. "This is the happiest day of my life!"

Mary gaped up at her, relief and elation flooding through her. "That's grand, missus! Oh, that's so grand!"

"Quick, get me some fresh flowers—we must make this place as cheerful as spring!" Diana laughed. She disappeared for a moment, and when she turned back again, she held a bouquet of faded white roses from a vase in the room. With hardly a pause she tossed the bouquet out of the window, and it fell in a graceful arc right into Mary's waiting hands.

BOOK V

All this I swallow, it tastes good, I like it well, it becomes mine.

—Walt Whitman, "Song of Myself"

Ginger

IF A YOUNG woman chose to keep something locked tight and guarded, she might use a heavy iron padlock. She would snap the lock into place and bury the key in the ocean, sure that the iron would hold forever. Time will rust the lock, however, and although it might look solid, a few sharp blows with a hammer will break it open.

The bouquet of flowers falling into Mary's hands was the final hammer strike. Mary crushed them against her chest to keep her heart from flying outward, but it was too late. She was breathless. Henry had won her in silence; in silence, unbeknownst to her, she had fallen in love. It could only be a calamity to her.

"Mary? Mary, where are you?" Rose called from the kitchen door.

Mary pressed the flowers against herself even tighter. She couldn't go inside. Henry was inside. She could not believe what had happened to her, in spite of everything, in spite of all her guards and defenses. She was hugely dismayed. Mary, who had no faith in the future, could not believe any good could come of falling in love. And yet she knew it had happened.

"Mary!"

"I'm just coming, Rose," she called back. Her heart lurched as Henry stepped out of the back door. She stood stricken and defenseless. She was sure everyone must know what she knew. Especially Henry.

But he only raised his hand in a wave and headed for the stable. Mary made her way gingerly to the kitchen door, like someone just wounded.

"Henry's just gone for Dr. Howard," Rose exclaimed as Mary stepped inside. "Mr. Dorsett's awake."

"Yes, I heard."

She looked down at the chair where Henry had been sitting and felt a cry forming. "Och, no, what's to be done?"

"Why, look sharp, make yourself useful," Rose scolded her. "Run along, there's a good girl."

"Yes, ma'am."

Mary let Rose shoo her from the kitchen and made her way to the sickroom. As she climbed the stairs, the light coming through the oval window seemed unusually bright, filling the upstairs hall with a brilliance that sparkled from prisms and mirrors and glass cases. A fly buzzed loudly against the window, and the chatter of swallows streaking past was sharp enough to make Mary turn and stare in amazement. The red runner on the floor gave off a sharp odor of wool as she walked across it.

From the door of the sickroom, she saw Mr. and Mrs. Dorsett beaming at each other. For a moment Mary looked at them in silence, and it seemed to her that their devotion created its own light. Shaken, Mary retrieved a stack of mail from the table in the hall and brought it to the bed.

"A very good morning to you, Mr. Dorsett. I'm sure you're wanting to know how the world fared without you—there's any number of letters I didn't know the answers to. Have you a mind to listen to some?"

"Without question. Missed me, did you?" Dorsett asked with a weak smile as she began opening his mail.

"Very much, sir. We've all been worried something terrible."

"And the damnedest thing is, I was worried, too,

only I couldn't say so! It was a very queer feeling," Dorsett said. He pushed himself up a bit higher on his pillows. "It's that feeling you have in a dream when you want to run but you can't move your legs. I couldn't speak!"

Diana Dorsett pressed her lips together and quickly looked away.

"Yes, very strange, sir, I'm sure," Mary agreed.

"I lost all my capacities to see and hear and feel. Can you imagine?"

Mary looked at him, a strange, pained smile on her lips. "I can, Mr. Dorsett. More than you know."

"But now I'm awake! Everything is changed now."

"Yes," Mary said. "Yes."

Mrs. Dorsett cleared her throat roughly. "Did Henry go for the doctor, Mary?"

A hot flush swept over Mary's face at the mention of Henry's name. She lowered her head over the mail. "Yes, ma'am. Sir, I did answer some of your letters myself. One was—"

"Yes, yes," Dorsett said. "I have no doubt you did a perfect job. I have every confidence in you."

"Do you?" Mary shook her head. "That's too generous of you, sir. It's the thankfulness at being back in health that makes you say so."

"Not at all. I believe you can do anything. You're an extraordinary girl."

Mary smiled. "Thank you, sir. It's good to have you back with us. Now, there's a small package here from Mr. Baird. Shall I open it?"

"Baird! Marvelous, open it indeed!" Dorsett crowed.

Mary busied herself with the package, pulling off the string and tearing the paper. There was a letter enclosed with a small box.

"I think it's candies, sir," she said. "It smells all of sugar."

"I'll wager it's more of that cursed ginger candy he's always sending us. Can't the man remember that we don't like it?" Dorsett appealed to his wife. "That man has no memory for anything but birds."

Diana laughed. "Just imagine being so preoccupied!"

"Oh, you're teasing me, don't think I don't know it," he said. "Mary, the candy is yours."

"Thank you, Mr. Dorsett," Mary said, slipping the box into the pocket of her apron. "Shall I read the letter?"

"Yes, do."

The next forty minutes were spent answering all of Dorsett's questions about what had happened in his "absence." Mary felt a strange lightness, a sense of being apart from herself. Dorsett believed she could do anything, and that flattered her more than she had expected. It made her proud to think she was extraordinary, and it almost tempted her to imagine what the future might hold. Every so often her pulse would race. She knew she was listening for the horse on the drive that would signal Henry's return.

But what she would do, if anything, what she would say, if anything, she didn't know. She thought she dreaded his return. Each sound made her strain to listen—the ticking clock, a distant footfall, the movement of the tree branches outside the open window. Several times she moved to rise and then sank back in her chair, shaking her head.

At the first clatter of hooves and carriage wheels she jumped so sharply that letters fluttered from her lap. "That'll be him—the doctor," she stammered, kneeling down to retrieve them.

"What's gotten into our Mary?" Mr. Dorsett asked his wife. "She's as jumpy as a cat."

"I'm sorry, sir, I'll just go let him in."

"I expect he can open a door without aid, but by all means, go on."

Now totally flustered, Mary hurried out of the room, grappling with the slithering heap of mail as she left. She felt utterly foolish. On the landing she paused, trying to compose herself.

From below came a muddle of voices. One was Dr. Howard's and one was a woman's, a voice Mary did not recognize. As she began to hurry down the stairs Mary promptly spilled all the letters. They cascaded down the steps ahead of her, and as she lunged for them she skidded on an envelope and only saved herself from falling headlong by grabbing at the banister.

"Mary and Joseph!" she cried. She clutched wildly at letters as she ran down to the hall.

"Good morning, doctor," she said with a breathless curtsy. "Mr. Dorsett is waiting for you."

"Thank you, Mary."

Dr. Howard strode past her up the stairs, leaving Mary alone with the visitor, an older woman in blue muslin and an elegant straw hat.

"I'm sorry, Mrs. Dorsett isn't taking any callers just at the moment," Mary said, mortified to have sworn in front of a friend of her employer's.

The older woman tipped her head to one side and regarded her for a moment. Mary felt a twinge of recognition and a thump of alarm.

"I didn't come to see Mrs. Dorsett, I came to visit with my son," the woman said. "I'm Mrs. Till, Henry's mother. And you must be the Mary we've heard so much about."

"Oh." Mary stared at her, and then at the mess of letters in her own hands. "Oh, dear."

With a jolt, Mary saw herself as the refined Mrs. Till must see her, a coarse Irish maid, a clumsy

Catholic girl from a saloon swearing on the stairs in front of a minister's wife. She knew what most genteel people thought of the Irish. She burned at having thought herself more than an ordinary maid, with a future as anything else.

"In fact, I'm glad to have a moment to speak with you alone, Mary," Mrs. Till continued. "May we sit somewhere for a moment? In here—I believe this is the music room," she said, leading the way.

Mary had no choice but to follow. She was afraid she was breaking every rule of propriety, receiving a caller in the house. And yet Mrs. Till was certainly a friend of the Dorsetts, even if her son was their man of all trades. With mounting confusion, Mary went into the music room, where Mrs. Till had taken a chair.

"Sit, Mary, please."

"Oh, no, I couldn't—" Mary began, and then promptly sat across from Henry's mother. She tried to make a neat stack of the letters in her lap, but her hands shook so much that it was useless. At last, she put the letters aside on the table and sat with her hands clasped together in her lap, feeling the hard edge of the candy box under her fingers. She couldn't look up. She had no doubt Henry's mother looked on her with disapproval and misgiving.

"I said that we had heard much about you, Mary."

"Yes, ma'am."

"From Henry. I was—I was *surprised* to find the two of you kept so much company together," Mrs. Till said carefully. "I never thought my son would—"

"Och, Mrs. Till, won't you have a sweet?" Mary rushed in, pulling the box from her pocket in desperation.

Mrs. Till gave the offered box a startled look. "Candied ginger? Oh, thank you, no. But please, you have one."

Miserable, Mary took a lump of candied ginger, knowing she could not keep Mrs. Till from speaking and putting her in her place. She bit into the candy and the spice was so strong that it almost brought tears to her eyes. She hadn't known ginger was hot.

Mrs. Till composed herself, folding her hands neatly in her lap and drawing breath as though for a difficult speech. "Mary, there is something I must say to you—"

"Please! Mrs. Till, there's no need," Mary cried, the ginger burning her tongue and her lips. "I beg your pardon for interrupting, but although I know myself for what I am, I can't bear to hear you say it.

I'm sure you're anxious that your son should not be entrapped by a common Irish housemaid. Never fear for that, ma'am. I know him to be the finest sort of person, and shouldn't wish to do him harm." She pressed her fingers against her mouth. The ginger was so hot that she wanted to spit it out. Mrs. Till's eyebrows were arched in surprise.

"I am that sorry if I shock you by speaking me mind," Mary continued, her accent broader by the moment. She was on the verge of tears. "And I'll warrant you didn't expect to hear so much from me, but I must set your mind at ease. I'll not throw myself at your son. Excuse me."

And without waiting for Mrs. Till's reply, Mary ran from the room, the taste of hot shame in her mouth.

Vinegar, Salt, and Sugar

PICKLING FUMES FILLED the kitchen like a sour fog. They caught in Mary's throat and made her cough. As Mary caught her breath, Rose dumped a handful of mustard seed into the pickling brine.

"Henry's mother is here to visit," Rose announced.

"I have just come from meeting her." Mary closed her eyes. "I've just been warned off."

"Warned off?" Rose gave the brine a hard stir. "What do you mean by that? Warned off what, and who did it?"

Mary didn't answer, but crossed the kitchen to

help with the pickling. She began placing jars in the huge kettle of water to sterilize. "Rose, I'm not used to the ways of working in a good house. I took fine manners and sweet tempers for more than they were."

"I don't pretend to understand you, young lady, but you won't find finer manners or sweeter tempers than Mr. and Mrs. Dorsett's, I'll tell you that." Rose crammed cucumber slices into a jar and ladled boiling vinegar over them.

"I have no doubt of that, Rose. But I am not used to being treated kindly, and it tempted me to think better of myself than what I am."

The cook patted Mary's arm. "There, you're a good girl, and a credit to your employer. I know you've given every satisfaction."

"Yes, as a good maid and secretary, I know." Bitterness and hurt pride welled up in Mary as she dunked the jars into the water. Pockets of air burst up to the surface like poisonous thoughts.

"And best keep in mind you'd have to look far to find a better position," Rose continued. "Or an easier cook to work under, I might add."

Mary tried to smile. "I count myself very lucky there, Rose."

"I should think so," Rose said comfortably. She raised a finger. "We're all very cozy here in the kitchen, I like to think, and of course we've got

Henry for company—why, he was brought up a gentleman and could still be one if he wished it, and I don't mind saying I can't understand why he wants to be a common working man. Not that there's any shame to it, but he was brought up for something finer."

Mary tasted sour bile in her throat. She turned away, wishing to drop the subject, but Rose was just warming up. "Mr. Till, that's Henry's father, you know—Mr. Till says Henry's lost his ideals and his faith in civilization, which I think is pure foolishness."

"Perhaps he's only lost the nerve to try," Mary muttered.

Rose put down the jar she was holding with a thump. "Mary Mehan, that's a terrible, cruel remark. Our Henry is a veteran and a hero and made a great sacrifice for our country. I'm ashamed of you."

"I'm sorry, Rose. I don't much like it myself."

"I'd like to know what he ever did to deserve such unkindness from a girl like you."

Mary felt her chin tremble. She couldn't understand herself what made her so savage and biting. "Nothing. He's only ever been good to me."

"There," Rose said triumphantly. "I knew it. He's goodness and kindness to everyone."

"Yes, that's true enough. He acts the same to

everyone. Why should I expect to be different from the rest?"

Rose threw her hands up. "You're sourer than the pickles today, Mary Mehan. I don't know what to do with you."

"I should never have come here in the first place."

"Then you're a mighty large fool *and* a sour one."

"Perhaps I am. Who am *I* to know otherwise?"

"You certainly woke up on the wrong side of the bed this morning."

Mary let out a deep breath. "Oh, didn't I just?"

They continued with the pickling in a vinegary silence until the door opened and Mrs. Dorsett came in, holding a handkerchief in front of her nose.

"My goodness, what a smell! Ladies, as soon as you're finished, I declare a holiday."

"Now, now, enough holidays, Mrs. Dorsett," Rose tutted. "We have a burden of work to do."

Diana smiled. "No, I insist. This is a joyful day, and I can only share my happiness with you all by letting you have a free day. You've worked very hard, especially my dear good nurse, Mary. Go on, now. Mrs. Till has left with Dr. Howard, and I understand from Henry there is some plan about a boat ride."

"Och, no—" Mary backed away. "I can't."

"Oh, yes you can." Diana took Mary's hand and pulled her forward. "This way."

Mary dragged her feet like a child as Mrs. Dorsett pulled her out into the hall. Through the open front door, she saw Mrs. Till climb into Dr. Howard's shay, and then lean out to give Henry one last kiss on the cheek. The doctor flicked the reins and the shay started off with a jerk. Henry raised his hand in farewell as the carriage bowled off down the drive. He carried a canvas satchel over one shoulder.

"Now, off with you both," Diana said, giving Mary a gentle shove.

"This is ridiculous," Mary whispered as the door shut behind her. She turned to the door, then turned back, shaking her hands in exasperation.

Mary could not explain her emotions, even to herself. She was as speechless as Henry. He did not speak; she could not. They were matched in silence.

Henry turned toward the house, and when he saw her, he inclined his head toward the lake with a smile. For a moment, Mary tried to find a way out of it. For a moment, she considered turning her back on him and marching back into the house.

But she couldn't. She couldn't. Mary went down the steps to join him, and together they headed for the boat house, side by side across the wide green lawn. Mary squinted at the sun as though looking for an answer. She hardly knew how she had come to be walking toward the lake with Henry, but there she was; all her senses told her—here was the green, green grass, there the sound of Henry's footsteps, there the cool watery breath of the lake, and there she was, too.

Henry opened the boat house door. Inside, the light from the water dappled and bounced off the walls and ceiling, and the two small boats bumped against each other as comfortably as two horses sharing a bit of pasture. There was a steady chuckle of waves from under the dock. Henry tossed his satchel into the dinghy and busied himself with the lines while Mary stepped carefully down into the boat and took the seat at the back. Henry untied the painter, stepped in, and shoved the dinghy backward with an oar. The little boat glided out into the sunshine.

While Henry rowed and the oars kept him from writing, there could be no conversation between them. Mary was glad of it. She felt the sun warm on her shoulders and back. She leaned over the side, letting one hand trail in the water as she watched her own reflection in the dark deep.

Mary could see her face and hear the soft splash

of the oars; she felt the cool water slip between her fingers and breathed in the fresh, fishy smell of it. A thin line of sweat beaded her lip, and when she ran her tongue over it, she tasted the salt.

She thought of the wide, salty ocean that she had crossed as a little girl. As she gazed into the water, she imagined she and Henry were rowing out onto it. Below her, faint veils of weeds slipped past, waving them onward. The round swell of the lake lifted them up and handed them forward. A gull passed over them, and tipped its head down to study them as it flew: two in a boat, alone on a wide, wide lake.

Sighing, Mary laid her head upon her folded arms and twisted so that she could watch Henry row. He leaned forward with the oars and pulled the boat across the lake, and the raised oars trailed lines of drops as they glided over the water. Because of Henry, Mary's solitary unhappiness was gone, and she could see, hear, feel, and smell and taste again. She loved him for it. The rest was nothing. The wounded pride, the anger, the fear, all these fell from her and sank like stones to the bottom of Lake Ontario. A fish darted in the deep and was gone.

Henry smiled when he noticed her watching him, and they regarded each other for a few moments as the boat reached for the horizon. Then Mary smiled and turned away, trailing her hand in the water again. She brought her fingers to her lips and tasted the clear, cool water, and then looked back the way they had come. The house lay behind them in the distance. "I did not know how far we had come," Mary said.

Henry shipped the oars and reached for the satchel, and from it took two apples. He bit one and held out the other. Mary shook her head no. For the first time in her life, she was flooded with peace. She tasted her own contentment and sighed, stretching her arms wide.

Henry's apple crunched loudly as he bit into it. He fished his notebook from his pocket, and wrote as he moved to sit close beside her. She read as he wrote.

You look as though you've just awoken from a magic sleep.

I have, she wrote. *At last I am awake.*

What were you dreaming?

I can't remember. It was a bad dream, but it's all faded now. There will be none but good dreams from now onward.

For me, too. In all my dreams, now, I can hear your voice. Singing.

Mary watched Henry take another bite of apple

as he wrote. She watched him chew. There was a drop of juice on his lip, and she knew she wanted to taste it, so she leaned toward him to kiss it from his mouth.

And it was very, very sweet.

Mrs. Jasper Dorsett
Lake Road
Grace Harbor

Dearest Diana,

It was all somewhat confusing at the beginning, but we have it clear at last. When I first met Mary, I was very distressed that she seemed so set against our dear Henry, when it was obvious to us all how he cared for her and we could all see what a change she'd made in him. Happily, it was only a misunderstanding on both our parts. I cannot tell you what a blessing I felt yesterday afternoon, watching them on the porch with their heads together as they passed notes back and forth—as though they could never say enough to each other. They are obviously planning something. I shall let you know what it is as soon as I know.

Fondly,

Emilia Till
August 1, 1865

Spencer F. Baird
Smithsonian Institution, Washington

Dear Baird,

How do you like the enclosed print? It's rather good, I think. My bluebirds posed for me like paid models at the Academy of Art. Now they have flown.

Speaking of which, my other birds have flown off, too. Mary Mehan, the girl you sent my way, turned out to be a most remarkable young woman, and she and my gardener have gone off to try being pioneers. I think we shall find Mary an asset to us in the future, her powers of observation being unusually keen and her interest in birds very good. If that fellow Whitman has any other protégées in his pocket, bring them on.

I'll send more prints very soon. I'm short-handed in the darkroom, as you now know. Next season I intend to try fixing the camera to the birds' box itself, although I haven't worked out yet the problem of illumination. I have all winter to puzzle out that conundrum as I regain my strength. My wife sends her greetings. We both hope this letter finds you in good health.

Your friend,

Jasper Dorsett
Grace Harbor, New York, September 17, 1865

. . . I have some small time now, Mr. Walt, to finish this letter just as the light is going. We have this last hour left Chicago behind us, and the train takes us into the West. The sun is setting there, and the corn in the meadows is full of gold and the wheeling birds. I let the window down, for we don't mind the cinders flying in at all, and would rather take the fresh air with cinders than the stale air without. Now the train goes faster and ever faster. I do like to put my head out the window and watch the sun sinking in its colors. Do you know, my Da was always on about the West, although to him it meant the West of Ireland—Clare and Galway and the rest—and so I grew from a girl with a dream of the golden West in my head. Now I go to the West of America. It lies before us, and we are flying to meet it.

I remain ever your friend,

Mary Mehan

Becoming Mary Mehan

TWO NOVELS

BY JENNIFER ARMSTRONG

A READERS GUIDE

Questions for Discussion

1. Why does Mairhe decide to change her name to Mary? How does this reflect her state of mind after the war?
2. In the first chapter of *The Dreams of Mairhe Mehan*, Mike is called a "damned Irish nigra." (p. 7) What other types of racial prejudice appear in the novel? Where do you see discrimination in today's society?
3. In *The Dreams of Mairhe Mehan*, Mary refers to the Fenians, a group of nineteenth-century nationalist revolutionaries. They supported the liberation of Ireland from Great Britain and the establishment of an independent Irish Republic. Mary says, "I'm not like Da. And I'm no Fenian. I've no plan to go back." (p. 19) Discuss the tension among Mary, Mike, and their father.
4. In *The Dreams of Mairhe Mehan*, the author interweaves battle scenes with a barroom dance. What are the connections between the two? Where are they discordant?
5. Discuss the many ways Mary imagines using the lace she makes—both literal and figurative. What makes the lace such a potent symbol for America?
6. At the conclusion of *The Dreams of Mairhe Mehan*, Mr. Walt (Whitman) quotes one of his poems, called "Starting from Paumanok," from *Leaves of Grass*, his autobiographical poem published in 1855. Mr. Walt says: "Listen dear son—listen America, daughter or son, It is a painful thing to love a man or woman to excess,

and yet it satisfies, it is great, But there is something else very great, it makes the whole coincide, It, magnificent, beyond materials, with continuous hands sweeps and provides for all." (p. 131) Discuss what this means to Mary.

7. Why do you think the author chooses to use Walt Whitman as a character?
8. What does Mary learn from Mr. Walt?
9. Mary describes her dreams as "the twilight between one world and another." (p. 3) How does she escape this dream world in *Mary Mehan Awake*?
10. How does the war affect Henry and Mary? How do their experiences both separate them from and connect them to other people?
11. Describe Mary's experience when she and Henry visit Niagara Falls in *Mary Mehan Awake*. Why is she surprised when they reach the Cave of the Winds at the bottom of the falls?
12. The author uses the following quotation from Walt Whitman's "Song of Myself" as the epigraph for Book III in *Mary Mehan Awake*: "Is this then a touch? quivering me to a new identity, / Flames and ether making a rush for my veins." (p. 217) How does this relate to Mary's friendship with Henry?
13. Why does Mr. Dorsett's illness frighten Mary?
14. Based on your readings of the dreams in these novels, do you think that dreams can influence your waking hours or that your waking hours can influence your dreams? Could both be true?
15. Mary writes a letter to Mr. Walt at the conclusion of *Mary Mehan Awake*. What is the author suggesting with Mary and Henry's journey to the West?

A NOTE FROM THE AUTHOR

First Light Studio

I wrote *The Dreams of Mairhe Mehan* in order to convey something of what I felt about the Civil War. It's a story of breakup and disorder and impossible hopes, and the form I chose to tell it in is a broken and disorderly one. It's all fragments and dreams. If the result is a successful marriage of form and content, I feel that I've done good work. It was certainly very hard work, and sometimes I found it difficult emotionally to sit down and make myself confront it.

When I was finished with *The Dreams of Mairhe Mehan*, I was drained and unhappy, and I had a sneaking suspicion that I owed something to my character. I had left her in the middle of a war, and I wished I could see her safely to a better place, but I felt too depleted to consider how I might do that. I left home and embarked on a long, solitary train journey into the wild north of Canada. I was so tired that I only took one book with me: It was a collection of essays about the pioneering naturalists of North America. As I watched the Canadian landscape flash past my window on the way up to Hudson Bay, I found that I *could* see how to lead Mairhe safely to a better place. The entire plot of *Mary Mehan Awake* came to me on that train ride; I had to scour the gift shop in the Winnipeg train station to find a spiral notebook so I could begin writing.

While *The Dreams of Mairhe Mehan* is narrated by Mairhe, I knew she could not narrate the sequel, because sleepwalkers cannot narrate stories. So I took the position of a naturalist-observer, watching and recording her progress. Like all Sleeping Beauty stories, this one has a prince to cut through the thorns to waken her. And I brought her to a happy ending at last.

—JENNIFER ARMSTRONG

IN HER OWN WORDS—
A CONVERSATION WITH JENNIFER ARMSTRONG

Q. What would you say are some of the obligations and opportunities of the historical novelist?

A. The most important issues of all are thoroughness and intellectual honesty. The more thoroughly you understand the values, the intellectual paradigms, the language, the literature, the popular culture, the high culture, the material culture, the technology, the superstitions, the cuisine, the politics, the prejudices, the mythologies, the worldview, and the manners of another age and another place, the more effective your work will be. And, I might add, the less likely you are to commit the intellectual blunder of ascribing contemporary ideas and values to a historical context. One of the hardest things about writing good historical fiction is gritting your teeth and letting your beloved characters say things and do things that could get them in big trouble in today's world. Things *were different* back then. *People* were different. *Ideas* were different. Don't be afraid that if your characters say something politically incorrect people will think you are saying this. Fiction is fiction, not autobiography.

Q. Has writing historical fiction changed your view of history?

A. It is comforting to think of history as a time line of hard facts, something that happened and that we can pin down, something that we categorize as factual, whereas fiction we categorize as nonfactual. However, it is only too clear to me that history is *not* something we can pin down. We circle around it and approach it from different angles, dart in at it, and grab parts of it. Real history is not factual. It is a story with many narrators and many endings, and the significance of any one event shifts and alters. *The Dreams of*

Mairhe Mehan explores this proposition. Readers should keep wondering, "Did that happen or is Mairhe making it up?" I wanted to suggest with this unreliable narrator that all of history's narrators are unreliable. Nevertheless, there's truth to be found somewhere in it.

Q. How do you go about injecting truth into a fictional story?

A. For *Becoming Mary Mehan*, I took what I knew about being Irish, poor, female, and an immigrant; I took what I knew about the Civil War, and I took what I knew about Whitman and his poetry; I took what I knew about race relations, President Lincoln, and the cadences of Irish poetry. I took all these things and more, and imagined a story where they all came together. But I could not make Whitman something he was not . . . in some strange dog-chasing-its-tail way, historical fiction takes all these things that *were* (the history) and turns something that *was not* (an imagined story) into something that *could have been*. That, I'd say, is the truth in storytelling.

Q. How do you make the history feel so personal?

A. As a writer of historical fiction, I bring whatever understanding I have about the human experience to imagine the effect of events on people's lives. Although I stand by what I said about understanding how things—people and cultures—were different, it is also true that human emotions and reactions don't change. The circumstances of those emotions and reactions might change, but hope is hope, fear is fear, wonder is wonder, no matter what century you're in. If I have felt those emotions, I can bring them to life in my characters.

Q. The American poet Walt Whitman appears in both novels as a friend and advisor for Mary Mehan. How did you go about creating dialogue for a real historical figure? What are the boundaries for a novelist here?

A. It is true that by placing real people—Walt Whitman, for example—in fictional scenes, I am inventing something untrue in the life of a known historical figure. There's a fine line to be walked here. I can't have Whitman in a scene cheering bloodthirstily for war and cussing the Rebs, because Whitman was not that kind of man. But I think I can be allowed to show him sitting by the side of a dying soldier, and consoling a frightened girl with hope of a greater good to come, because Whitman was *that* kind of man. He *could* have befriended an Irish girl in Washington, and he certainly kept watch over many a dying soldier. These scenes cannot be said to be authentic, because they are invented, but I believe they are entirely plausible. I tried to limit the number of scenes with Whitman, for fear of going too far and taking liberties with a man whom so many people know and admire. I considered it something in the nature of asking a favor of a generous friend: I didn't want to get greedy and ask too much.

Q. Having written both historical fiction and historical nonfiction, how would you describe the difference?

A. When I write a novel, I am *fictionalizing* historical events; when I write nonfiction, I am *dramatizing* historical events. My responsibility is twofold in each case: to write a good story and to make the history that surrounds it legible. The emphasis in the case of historical fiction is to tell a good story first, and then to be careful that it is well supported by the history. In the case of historical nonfiction, the priority is to make the history legible, and then to make sure it's a darn good story. Otherwise who's going to want to read it?

Q. How do you begin your research? Do you work differently if you are creating a piece of fiction or nonfiction?

A. Whenever possible, these are the sources I like to study: diaries, letters, newspapers, commercial advertisements, political speeches, sermons, songs, children's stories and other pedagogical material, recipes, wills and household inventories, travelogues, maps, manuals of advice, architectural drawings, cargo manifests, menus, photographs, farmers' almanacs, paintings, dress patterns, help-wanted ads, court transcripts, medical handbooks, et cetera. You can learn so much about a culture from studying these things. I don't research differently for fiction and nonfiction, because in both cases, the goal is to absorb as much as possible about the period in order to make it come to life on the page.

Q. Do you travel to the sites you write about? Did you visit Washington, D.C., before writing *The Dreams of Mairhe Mehan* or Lake Ontario before writing *Mary Mehan Awake*?

A. No, I did not go to Washington, D.C., because the Capital City I was writing about no longer exists. Travel can be a part of gathering insights into the past, but there are pitfalls there, too.

If you can't remove the contemporary overlay from a city you are looking at, it will be hard to imagine it without cars or without tall buildings. If you are researching a specific place and it has a lot of human artifacts, it might be better to use historical photos, if possible, or paintings, or written descriptions. This is what I was able to do with Washington; there are many, many photographs of the capital during the war, so this is what I used for location research.

A natural setting may be a different story. Although Niagara Falls has changed to a degree since the nineteenth century, the power of this natural wonder is so extraordinary that it was very helpful for me to go there, to feel the thunder coming up through my feet and shaking my bones, and to know that it would have been *even more so* before the hydroelectric plants diverted so much of the Niagara River. By the same token, Lake Ontario itself hasn't altered very much. There is still much undeveloped shoreline, and there are still many small towns that haven't changed significantly in a hundred years.

Travel is a useful tool for location research, but it should be done with these caveats: that you should only do it if you can make yourself *not see* the modern age when you are looking or if you cannot find historical images of the setting.

Q. Do you have other sources of inspiration? Where do you look for ideas for your work?

A. If you want to be good at writing about history, your interest in history should be ever-present and eclectic. Reading history should be something you do all the time, not just when you're working on a project. Read widely, read often. I refer to this as casting the net; when you cast the net widely and often, you'll have a bountiful catch. The first thing you'll catch is story ideas. The second thing you'll catch is the unexpected, unlooked-for echo of something you are working on. Another sort of net-casting I try to practice as much as possible is jumping at opportunities that will take me out of the twenty-first century. I've been to Civil War battle reenactments and been shocked and shaken by how loud a rifle salvo is and by how quickly the air is clouded with sharp, eye-stinging smoke.

Q. How do you structure your writing time? What is your typical workday?

A. My typical workday is to do e-mail in the morning, and maybe do errands or go to the library. Then by 11 A.M. at the latest, I get to my office and work. Not all my work is writing books—sometimes I have to spend time writing a speech or an article for a magazine, or making arrangements with a school to do an author visit there. Sometimes I have to talk on the phone with my editor about one of the projects I'm working on. I try to keep pretty normal business hours, which means I quit by five or six and that's it for the day.

Q. When did you know you wanted to be a writer?

A. By the time I was in first grade, I knew I was going to be an author. The only time I briefly considered a different career was in sixth grade, when we were studying ancient Egypt in social studies and I decided to become an archaeologist. I loved those mummies. My enthusiasm for a life in archaeology eventually waned, however; I was always, first and last, an author.

Kit's Wilderness

DAVID ALMOND

0-440-41605-1

Kit Watson and John Askew look for the childhood ghosts of their long-gone ancestors in the mines of Stoneygate.

Skellig

DAVID ALMOND

0-440-22908-1

Michael feels helpless because of his baby sister's illness, until he meets a creature called Skellig.

Heaven Eyes

DAVID ALMOND

0-440-22910-3

Erin Law and her friends in the orphanage are labeled Damaged Children. They run away one night, traveling downriver on a raft. What they find on their journey is stranger than you can imagine.

Available October 2002

Becoming Mary Mehan—Two Novels

JENNIFER ARMSTRONG

0-440-22961-8

Set against the events of the American Civil War, *The Dreams of Mairhe Mehan* depicts an Irish immigrant girl and her family who are struggling to find their place in the war-torn country. *Mary Mehan Awake* takes up Mary's story after the war, when she must begin a journey of renewal.

Forgotten Fire

ADAM BAGDASARIAN

0-440-22917-0

In 1915, Vahan Kenderian is living a life of privilege when his world is shattered by the Turkish-Armenian War.

Ghost Boy

IAIN LAWRENCE

0-440-41668-X

Fourteen-year-old Harold Kline is an albino—an outcast. When the circus comes to town, Harold runs off to join it in hopes of discovering who he is and what he wants in life. Is he a circus freak or just a normal guy?

Gathering Blue

LOIS LOWRY

0-440-22949-9

Lamed and suddenly orphaned, Kira is mysteriously removed to live in the palatial Council Edifice, where she is expected to use her gifts as a weaver to do the bidding of the all-powerful Guardians.

Available September 2002

The Giver

LOIS LOWRY

0-440-23768-8

Jonas's world is perfect. Everything is under control. There is no war or fear or pain. There are no choices, until Jonas is given an opportunity that will change his world forever.

Available September 2002

Both Sides Now

RUTH PENNEBAKER

0-440-22933-2

A compelling look at breast cancer through the eyes of a mother and daughter. Liza must learn a few life lessons from her mother, Rebecca, about the power of family.

Available July 2002

Her Father's Daughter

MOLLIE POUPENEY

0-440-22879-4

As she matures from a feisty tomboy of seven to a spirited young woman of fourteen, Maggie discovers that the only constant in her life of endless new homes and new faces is her ever-emerging sense of herself.

Available June 2002

The Baboon King

ANTON QUINTANA

0-440-22907-3

Neither Morengáru's father's Masai tribe nor his mother's Kikuyu tribe accepts him. Banished from both tribes, Morengáru encounters a baboon troop and faces a fight with the simian king.

Holes

LOUIS SACHAR

0-440-22859-X

Stanley has been unjustly sent to a boys' detention center, Camp Green Lake. But there's more than character improvement going on at the camp—the warden is looking for something.

Memories of Summer

RUTH WHITE

0-440-22921-9

In 1955, thirteen-year-old Lyric describes her older sister Summer's descent into mental illness, telling Summer's story with humor, courage, and love.

Available May 2002

OTHER BOOKS BY JENNIFER ARMSTRONG

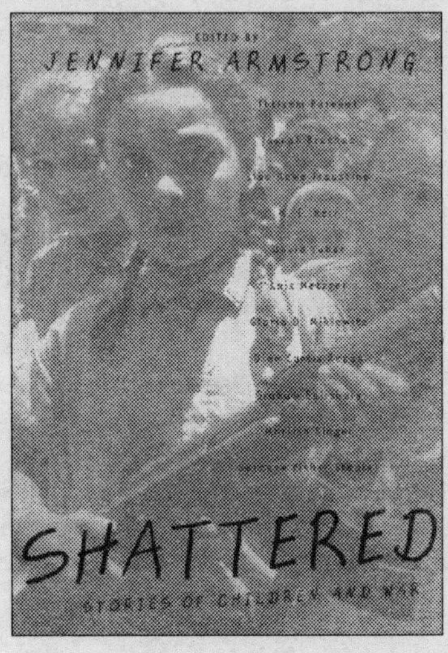

Shattered

Stories of Children and War

EDITED BY JENNIFER ARMSTRONG

0-375-81112-5

This collection, written by twelve noted young adult authors, examines all of war's implications for young people—from those caught in the line of fire to the children of veterans of wars long past.

Critically acclaimed author Jennifer Armstrong brings together these powerful voices in young people's literature to explore the realities of war, including stories by M. E. Kerr, Suzanne Fisher Staples, Joseph Bruchac, Marilyn Singer, Graham Salisbury, and many more. The settings vary widely—the Soviet invasion of Afghanistan, an attempted coup in Venezuela, the American Civil War, crises in the Middle East—but the effects are largely the same. In war, no life is left untouched. In war, all lives are shattered.

OTHER BOOKS BY JENNIFER ARMSTRONG

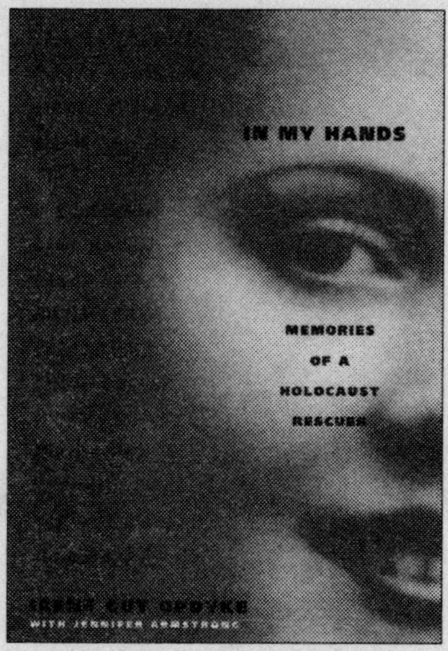

In My Hands

Memories of a Holocaust Rescuer

IRENE GUT OPDYKE

WITH JENNIFER ARMSTRONG

0-679-89181-1

You must understand that I did not become a resistance fighter, a smuggler of Jews, a defier of the SS and the Nazis all at once. One's first steps are always small: I had begun by hiding food under a fence.

Irene Gut was just seventeen when the war began: a Polish patriot, a student nurse, and a good Catholic girl. As the war progressed, the soldiers of two countries stripped her of all she loved—her family, her home, her innocence—but the degradations only strengthened her will. Irene was forced to work for the German army, but her blond hair, blue eyes, and youth bought her the relatively safe job of waitress in an officers' dining room. She would use this Aryan mask as both a shield and a sword. When she was made the housekeeper of a Nazi major, she successfully hid twelve Jews in the basement of his home until the Germans' defeat.

OTHER BOOKS BY JENNIFER ARMSTRONG

Shipwreck at the Bottom of the World

***The Extraordinary True Story of Shackleton and the* Endurance**

0-375-81049-8

In August 1914, Ernest Shackleton and twenty-seven men sailed from England in an attempt to become the first team of explorers to cross Antarctica. Five months later and still a hundred miles from land, their ship, *Endurance*, became trapped in ice. The expedition survived another five months camping on ice floes, followed by a perilous journey through stormy seas to the remote and unvisited Elephant Island. In a dramatic climax to this amazing survival story, Shackleton and five others navigated eight hundred miles of treacherous open ocean in a twenty-foot boat to fetch a rescue ship.